Bed Time Stories: Uncle Wiggily in the Woods

Howard R. Garis

Illustrated by Louis Wisa

She put her sled on the slanting tree,
sat down and Jillie gave her a little push.

BEDTIME STORIES

Uncle Wiggily in the Woods

BY

HOWARD R. GARIS

Author Of "SAMMIE AND SUSIE LITTLETAIL," "UNCLE
WIGGILY AND MOTHER GOOSE," "THE BEDTIME SERIES OF
ANIMAL STORIES," "THE DADDY SERIES," ETC.

ILLUSTRATED BY LOUIS WISA

A. L. BURT COMPANY

PUBLISHERS — — — — — — NEW YORK

CONTENTS

ILLUSTRATIONS

She put her sled on the slanting tree, sat down and Jillie gave her a little push . . . . . . *Frontispiece*

Down toppled Uncle Wiggily's hat, not in the least hurt.

As they passed a high rock, out from behind it jumped the bad old tail-pulling monkey.

The tree barked and roared so like a lion that the foxes were frightened and were glad enough to run away.

Up, up and up into the air blew the kite and, as the string was tangled around the babboon's paws, it took him up with it.

"Ker-sneezio! Ker-snitzio! Ker-choo!" he sneezed as the powder from the puff balls went up his nose and into his eyes.

Jackie was so surprised that he opened his mouth.

Before Uncle Wiggily could stop himself he had run into the bush.

STORY I

UNCLE WIGGILY AND THE WILLOW TREE

"Well, it's all settled!" exclaimed Uncle Wiggily Longears, the rabbit gentleman, one day, as he hopped up the steps of his hollow stump bungalow where Nurse Jane Fuzzy Wuzzy, his muskrat lady housekeeper, was fanning herself with a cabbage leaf tied to her tail. "It's all settled."

"What is?" asked Miss Fuzzy Wuzzy. "You don't mean to tell me anything has happened to you?" and she looked quite anxious.

"No, I'm all right," laughed Uncle Wiggily, "and I hope you are the same. What I meant was that it's all settled where we are going to spend our vacation this Summer."

"Oh, tell me where!" exclaimed the muskrat lady clapping her paws, anxious like.

"In a hollow stump bungalow, just like this, but in the woods instead of in the country," answered Uncle Wiggily.

"Oh, that *will* be fine!" cried Miss Fuzzy Wuzzy. "I love the woods. When are we to go?"

"Very soon now," answered the bunny gentleman uncle. "You may begin to pack up as quickly as you please."

And Nurse Jane and Uncle Wiggily moved to the woods very next day and his adventures began.

I guess most of you know about the rabbit gentleman and his muskrat lady housekeeper who nursed him when he was ill with the rheumatism. Uncle Wiggily had lots and lots of adventures, about which I have told you in the books before this one.

1

He had traveled about seeking his fortune, he had even gone sailing in his airship, and once he met Mother Goose and all her friends from Old King Cole down to Little Jack Horner.

Uncle Wiggily had many friends among the animal boys and girls. There was Sammie and Susie Littletail, the rabbits, who have a book all to themselves; just as have Jackie and Peetie Bow Wow, the puppy dog boys, and Jollie and Jillie Longtail, the mice children.

"And I s'pose we'll meet all your friends in the woods, won't we, Uncle Wiggily?" asked Nurse Jane, as they moved from the old hollow stump bungalow to the new one.

"Oh, yes, I s'pose so, of course," he laughed in answer, as he pulled his tall silk hat more tightly down on his head, fastened on his glasses and took his red, white and blue striped barber pole rheumatism crutch that Nurse Jane had gnawed for him out of a cornstalk.

So, once upon a time, not very many years ago, as all good stories should begin, Uncle Wiggily and Nurse Jane found themselves in the woods. It was lovely among the trees, and as soon as the rabbit gentleman had helped Miss Fuzzy Wuzzy put the hollow stump bungalow to rights he started out for a walk.

"I want to see what sort of adventures I shall have in the woods," said Mr. Longears as he hopped along.

Now in these woods lived, among many other creatures good and bad, two skillery-scalery alligators who were not exactly friends of the bunny uncle. But don't let that worry you, for though the alligators, and other unpleasant animals, may, once in a while, make trouble for Uncle Wiggily, I'll never really let them hurt him. I'll fix that part all right!

So, one day, the skillery-scalery alligator with the humps on his tail, and his brother, another skillery-scalery chap, whose tail was double jointed, were taking a walk through the woods together just as Uncle Wiggily was doing.

"Brother," began the hump-tailed 'gator (which I call him for short), "brother, wouldn't you like a nice rabbit?"

"Indeed I would," answered the double-jointed tail 'gator, who could wobble his flippers both ways. "And I know of no nicer rabbit than Uncle Wiggily Longears."

"The very same one about whom I was thinking!" exclaimed the other alligator. "Let's catch him!"

"That's what we'll do!" said the double-jointed chap. "We'll hide in the woods until he comes along, as he does every day, and the we'll jump out and grab him. Oh, you yum-yum!"

"Fine!" grunted his brother. "Come on!"

Off they crawled through the woods, and pretty soon they came to a willow tree, where the branches grew so low down that they looked like a curtain that had unwound itself off the roller, when the cat hangs on it.

"This is the place for us to hide—by the weeping willow tree," said the skillery-scalery alligator with bumps on his tail.

"The very place," agreed his brother.

So they hid behind the thick branches of the tree, which had leafed out for early spring, and there the two bad creatures waited.

Just before this Uncle Wiggily himself had started out from his hollow stump bungalow to walk in the woods and across the fields, as he did every day.

"I wonder what sort of an adventure I shall have this time?" he said to himself. "I hope it will be a real nice one."

Oh! If Uncle Wiggily had known what was in store for him, I think he would have stayed in his hollow stump bungalow. But never mind, I'll make it all come out right in the end, you see if I don't. I don't know just how I'm going to do it, yet, but I'll find a way, never fear.

Uncle Wiggily hopped on and on, now and then swinging his red-white-and-blue-striped rheumatism crutch like a cane, because he felt so young and spry and spring-like. Pretty soon he came to the willow tree. He was sort of looking up at it, wondering if a nibble of some of the green leaves would not do him good, when, all of a sudden, out jumped the two bad alligators and grabbed the bunny gentleman.

"Now we have you!" cried the humped-tail 'gator.

"And you can't get away from us," said the other chap—the double-jointed tail one.

"Oh, please let me go!" begged Uncle Wiggily, but they hooked their claws in his fur, and pulled him back under the tree, which held its branches so low. I told you it was a weeping willow tree, and just now it was weeping, I think, because Uncle Wiggily was in such trouble.

"Let's see now," said the double-jointed tail alligator. "I'll carry this rabbit home, and then—"

"You'll do nothing of the sort!" interrupted the other, and not very politely, either. "I'll carry him myself. Why, I caught him as much as you did!"

"Well, maybe you did, but I saw him first."

"I don't care! It was my idea. I first thought of this way of catching him!"

And then those two alligators disputed, and talked very unpleasantly, indeed, to one another.

But, all the while, they kept tight hold of the bunny uncle, so he could not get away.

"Well," said the double-jointed tail alligator after a while, "we must settle this one way or the other. Am I to carry him to our den, or you?"

"Me! I'll do it. If you took him you'd keep him all for yourself. I know you!"

"No, I wouldn't! But that's just what you'd do. I know you only too well. No, if I can't carry this rabbit home myself, you shan't!"

"I say the same thing. I'm going to have my rights."

Now, while the two bad alligators were talking this way they did not pay much attention to Uncle Wiggily. They held him so tightly in their claws that he could not get away, but he could use his own paws, and, when the two bad creatures were talking right in each other's face, and using big words, Uncle Wiggily reached up and cut off a piece of willow wood with the bark on.

And then, still when the 'gators were disputing, and not looking, the bunny uncle made himself a whistle out of the willow tree stick. He loosened the bark, which came off like a kid glove, and then he cut a place to blow his breath in, and another place to let the air out and so on, until he had a very fine whistle indeed, almost as loud-blowing as those the policemen have to stop the automobiles from splashing mud on you so a trolley car can bump into you.

"I'll tell you what we'll do," said the hump-tail alligator at last. "Since you won't let me carry him home, and I won't let you, let's both carry him together. You take hold of him on one side, and I'll take the other."

"Good!" cried the second alligator.

"Oh, ho! I guess not!" cried the bunny uncle suddenly. "I guess you won't either, or both of you take me off to your den. No, indeed!"

"Why not?" asked the hump-tailed 'gator, sort of impolite like and sarcastic.

"Because I'm going to blow my whistle and call the police!" went on the bunny uncle. "Toot! Toot! Tootity-ti-toot-toot!"

And then and there he blew such a loud, shrill blast on his willow tree whistle that the alligators had to put their paws over their ears. And when they did that they had to let go of bunny uncle. He had his tall silk hat down over his ears, so it didn't matter how loudly he blew the whistle. He couldn't hear it.

"Toot! Toot! Tootity-toot-toot!" he blew on the willow whistle.

"Oh, stop! Stop!" cried the hump-tailed 'gator.

"Come on, run away before the police come!" said his brother. And out from under the willow tree they both ran, leaving Uncle Wiggily safely behind.

"Well," said the bunny gentleman as he hopped along home to his bungalow, "it is a good thing I learned, when a boy rabbit, how to make whistles." And I think so myself.

So if the vinegar jug doesn't jump into the molasses barrel and turn its face sour like a lemon pudding, I'll tell you next about Uncle Wiggily and the winter green.

STORY II

UNCLE WIGGILY AND THE WINTERGREEN

Uncle Wiggily Longears, the nice old gentleman rabbit, knocked on the door of the hollow tree in the woods where Johnnie and Billie Bushytail, the two little squirrel boys, lived.

"Come in!" invited Mrs. Bushytail. So Uncle Wiggily went in.

"I thought I'd come around and see you," he said to the squirrel lady. "I'm living in the woods this Summer and just now I am out taking a walk, as I do every day, and I hoped I might meet with an adventure. But, so far, I haven't. Do you know where I could find an adventure, Mrs. Bushytail?"

"No, I'm sorry to say I don't, Uncle Wiggily," answered the squirrel lady. "But I wish you could find something to make my little boy Billie feel better."

"Why, is he ill?" asked the bunny uncle, surprised like, and he looked across the room where Billy Bushytail was curled up in a big rocking chair, with his tail held over his head like an umbrella, though it was not raining.

"No, Billie isn't ill," said Mrs. Bushytail. "But he says he doesn't know what to do to have any fun, and I am afraid he is a little peevish."

"Oh, that isn't right," said Mr. Longears. "Little boys, whether they are squirrels, rabbits or real children, should try to be jolly and happy, and not peevish."

"How can a fellow be happy when there's no fun?" asked Billie, sort of cross-like. "My brother Johnnie got out of school early, and he and the other animal boys have gone off to play where I can't find them. I

7

had to stay in, because I didn't know my nut-cracking lesson, and now I can't have any fun. Oh, dear! I don't care!"

Billie meant, I suppose, that he didn't care what he said or did, and that isn't right. But Uncle Wiggily only pinkled his twink nose. No, wait just a moment if you please. He just twinkled his pink nose behind the squirrel boy's back, and then the bunny uncle said:

"How would you like to come for a walk in the woods with me, Billie?"

"Oh, that will be nice!" exclaimed the squirrel lady. "Do go, Billie."

"No, I don't want to!" chattered the boy squirrel, most impolitely.

"Oh, that isn't at all nice," said Mrs. Bushy-tail. "At least thank Uncle Wiggily for asking you."

"Oh, excuse me, Uncle Wiggily," said Billie, sorrylike. "I do thank you. But I want very much to have some fun, and there's no fun in the woods. I know all about them. I know every tree and bush and stump. I want to go to a new place."

"Well, new places are nice," said the bunny uncle, "but old ones are nice, too, if you know where to look for the niceness. Now come along with me, and we'll see if we can't have some fun. It is lovely in the woods now."

"I won't have any fun there," said Billie, crossly. "The woods are no good. Nothing good to eat grows there."

"Oh, yes there does—lots!" laughed Uncle Wiggily. "Why the nuts you squirrels eat grow in the woods."

"Yes, but there are no nuts now," spoke the squirrel boy. "They only come in the Fall."

"Well, come, scamper along, anyhow," invited Uncle Wiggily. "Who knows what may happen? It may even be an adventure. Come along, Billie."

So, though he did not care much about it, Billie went. Uncle Wiggily showed the squirrel boy where the early spring flowers were coming up, and how the Jacks, in their pulpits, were getting ready to preach sermons to the trees and bushes.

"Hark! What's that?" asked Billie, suddenly, hearing a noise.

"What does it sound like?" asked Uncle Wiggily.

"Like bells ringing."

"Oh, it's the bluebells—the bluebell flowers," answered the bunny uncle.

"Why do they ring?" asked the little boy squirrel.

"To call the little ants and lightning bugs to school," spoke Uncle Wiggily, and Billy smiled. He was beginning to see that there were more things in the woods than he had dreamed of, even if he had scampered here and there among the trees ever since he was a little squirrel chap.

On and on through the woods went the bunny uncle and Billie. They picked big, leafy ferns to fan themselves with, and then they drank with green leaf-cups from a spring of cool water.

But no sooner had Billie taken the cold water than he suddenly cried:

"Ouch! Oh, dear! Oh, my, how it hurts!"

"What is it?" asked Uncle Wiggily. "Did you bite your tongue or step on a thorn?"

"It's my tooth," chattered Billie. "The cold water made it ache again. I need to go to Mr. Stubtail, the bear dentist, who will pull it out with his long claws. But I've been putting it off, and putting it off, and now—Oh, dear, how it aches! Wow!"

"I'll cure it for you!" said Uncle Wiggily. "Just walk along through the woods with me and I'll soon stop your aching tooth."

"How can you?" asked Billie, holding his paw to his jaw to warm the aching tooth, for heat will often stop pain. "There isn't anything here in the woods to cure toothache; is there?"

"I think we shall find something," spoke the bunny uncle.

"Well, I wish we could find it soon!" cried Billie, "for my tooth hurts very much. Ouch!" and he hopped up and down, for the toothache was of the jumping kind.

"Ah, ha! Here we have it!" cried Uncle Wiggily, as he stooped over some shiny green leaves, growing close to the ground, and he pulled some of them up. "Just chew these leaves a little and let them rest inside your mouth near the aching tooth," said Mr. Longears. "I think they will help you, Billie."

So Billie chewed the green leaves. They smarted and burned a little, but when he put them near his tooth they made it nice and warm and soon the ache all stopped.

"What was that you gave me, Uncle Wiggily?" Billie asked.

"Wintergreen," answered Uncle Wiggily. "It grows in the woods, and is good for flavoring candy, as well as for stopping toothache."

"I am glad to know that," said Billie. "The woods are a nicer place than I thought, and there is ever so much more in them than I dreamed. Thank you, Uncle Wiggily."

So, as his toothache was all better, Billie had good fun in the woods with the bunny uncle, until it was time to go home. And in the next story, if the top doesn't fly off the coffee pot and let the baked potato hide away from the egg-beater, when they play tag, I'll tell you about Uncle Wiggily and the slippery elm.

STORY III

UNCLE WIGGILY AND THE SLIPPERY ELM

"Where are you going, Uncle Wiggily?" asked Nurse Jane Fuzzy Wuzzy, the muskrat lady housekeeper, as she saw the rabbit gentleman standing on the front steps of his hollow stump bungalow in the woods one morning. "Where are you going?"

"Oh, just for a walk through the forest," spoke the bunny uncle. "It is so nice in the woods, with the flowers coming up, and the leaves getting larger and greener every day, that I just love to walk there."

"Well," said Nurse Jane with a laugh, "if you happen to see a bread-tree in the woods, bring home a loaf for supper."

"I will," promised Uncle Wiggily. "You know, Nurse Jane, there really are trees on which bread fruit grows, though not in this country. But I can get you a loaf of bread at the five and ten cent store, I dare say."

"Do, please," asked the muskrat lady. "And if you see a cocoanut tree you might bring home a cocoanut cake for supper."

"Oh, my!" laughed the rabbit gentleman. "I'm afraid there are no cocoanut trees in my woods. I could bring you home a hickory nut cake, perhaps."

"Well, whatever you like," spoke Nurse Jane. "But don't get lost, whatever you do, and if you meet with an adventure I hope it will be a nice one."

"So do I," Uncle Wiggily said, as he hopped off, leaning on his red, white and blue stripped [Transcriber's note: striped?] rheumatism crutch which Nurse Jane had gnawed for him out of a cornstalk.

12

The old rabbit gentleman had not gone very far before he met Dr. Possum walking along in the woods, with his satchel of medicine on his tail, for Dr. Possum cured all the ill animals, you know.

"What in the world are you doing, Dr. Possum?" asked Uncle Wiggily, as he saw the animal doctor pulling some bark off a tree. "Are you going to make a canoe, as the Indians used to do?"

"Oh, no," answered Dr. Possum. "This is a slippery elm tree. The underside of the bark, next to the tree, and the tree itself, is very slippery when it is wet. Very slippery indeed."

"Well, I hope you don't slip," said Uncle Wiggily, kindly.

"I hope so, too," Dr. Possum said. "But I am taking this slippery elm bark to mix with some of the bitter medicine I have to give Billie Wagtail, the goat boy. When I put some bark from the slippery elm tree in Billie's medicine it will slip down his throat so quickly that he will never know he took it."

"Good!" cried Uncle Wiggily, laughing. Then the bunny uncle went close to the tree, off which Dr. Possum was taking some bark, and felt of it with his paw. The tree was indeed as slippery as an icy sidewalk slide on Christmas eve.

"My!" exclaimed Mr. Longears. "If I tried to climb up that tree I'd do nothing but slip down."

"That's right," said Dr. Possum. "But I must hurry on now to give Billie Wagtail his medicine."

So Dr. Possum went on his way and Uncle Wiggily hopped along until, pretty soon, he heard a rustling in the bushes, and a voice said:

"But, Squeaky-Eeky dear, I can't find any snow hill for you to ride down on your sled. The snow is all gone, you see. It is Spring now."

"Oh, dear!" cried another voice. "Such a lot of trouble. Oh, dear! Oh, dear!"

"Ha! Trouble!" said Uncle Wiggily to himself. "This is where I come in. I must see if I cannot help them."

He looked through the bushes, and there he saw Jillie Longtail, the little girl mouse, and with her was Squeaky-Eeky, the cousin mouse. And Squeaky-Eeky had a small sled with her.

"Why, what's the matter?" asked Uncle Wiggily, for he saw that Squeaky-Eeky had been crying. "What is the matter, little mice?"

"Oh, hello. Uncle Wiggily!" cried Jillie. "I don't know what to do with my little cousin mouse. You see she wants to slide down hill on her Christmas sled, but there isn't any snow on any of the hills now."

"No, that's true, there isn't," said the bunny uncle. "But, Squeaky, why didn't you slide down hill in the Winter, when there was snow?"

"Because, I had the mouse-trap fever, then," answered Squeaky-Eeky, "and I couldn't go out. But now I am all better and I can be out, and oh, dear! I do so much want a ride down hill on my sled. Boo, hoo!"

"Don't cry, Squeaky, dear," said Jillie. "If there is no snow you can't slide down hill, you know."

"But I want to," said the little cousin mouse, unreasonable like.

"But you can't; so please be nice," begged Jillie.

"Oh, dear!" cried Squeaky. "I do so much want to slide down hill on my sled."

"And you shall!" suddenly exclaimed Uncle Wiggily. "Come with me, Squeaky."

"Why, Uncle Wiggily!" cried Jillie. "How can you give Squeaky a slide down hill when there is no snow? You need a slippery snow hill for sleigh-riding."

"I am not so sure of that," spoke Uncle Wiggily, with a smile. "Let us see."

Off through the woods he hopped, with Jillie and Squeaky following. Pretty soon Uncle Wiggily came to a big tree that had fallen down, one end being raised up higher than the other, like a hill, slanting.

With his strong paws and his sharp teeth, the rabbit gentleman began peeling the bark off the tree, showing the white wood underneath.

"What are you doing, Uncle Wiggily?" asked Jillie.

"This is a slippery elm tree, and I am making a hill so Squeaky-Eeky can slide down," answered the bunny uncle. "Underneath the bark the trunk of the elm tree is very slippery. Dr. Possum told me so. See how my paw slips!" And indeed it did, sliding down the sloping tree almost as fast as you can eat a lollypop.

Uncle Wiggily took off a lot of bark from the elm tree, making a long, sliding, slippery place.

"Now, try that with your sled, Squeaky-Eeky," said the bunny uncle. And the little cousin mouse did. She put her sled on the slanting tree, sat down and Jillie gave her a little push. Down the slippery elm tree went Squeaky as fast as anything, coming to a stop in a pile of soft leaves.

"Oh, what a lovely slide!" cried Squeaky. "You try it, Jillie." And the little mouse girl did.

"Who would think," she said, "that you could slide down a slippery elm tree? But you can."

Then she and Squeaky took turns sliding down hill, even though there was no snow, and the slippery elm tree didn't mind it a bit, but rather liked it.

And if the coal man doesn't take away our gas shovel to shoot some tooth powder into the wax doll's pop gun, I'll tell you next about Uncle Wiggily and the sassafras.

STORY IV

UNCLE WIGGILY AND THE SASSAFRAS

"Uncle Wiggily! Uncle Wiggily! Get up!" called Nurse Jane Fuzzy Wuzzy, the muskrat lady housekeeper, as she stood at the foot of the stairs of the hollow stump bungalow and called up to the rabbit gentleman one morning.

"Hurry down, Mr. Longears," she went on. "This is the last day I am going to bake buckwheat cakes, and if you want some nice hot ones, with maple sugar sauce on, you'd better hurry."

No answer came from the bunny uncle.

"Why, this is strange," said Nurse Jane to herself. "I wonder if anything can have happened to him? Did he have an adventure in the night? Did the bad skillery-scalery alligator, with humps on its tail, carry him off?"

Then she called again:

"Uncle Wiggily! Uncle Wiggily! Aren't you going to get up? Come down to breakfast. Aren't you going to get up and come down?"

"No, Miss Fuzzy Wuzzy," replied the bunny uncle, "not to give you a short answer, I am not going to get up, or come down or eat breakfast or do anything," and Mr. Longears spoke as though his head was hidden under the bed clothes, which it was.

"Oh, Uncle Wiggily, whatever is the matter?" asked Nurse Jane, surprised like and anxious.

"I don't feel at all well," was the answer. "I think I have the epizootic, and I don't want any breakfast."

17

"Oh, dear!" cried Nurse Jane. "And all the nice cakes I have baked. I know what I'll do," she said to herself. "I'll call in Dr. Possum. Perhaps Uncle Wiggily needs some of the roots and herbs that grow in the woods—wintergreen, slippery elm or something like that. I'll call Dr. Possum."

And when the animal doctor came he looked at the bunny uncle's tongue, felt of his ears, and said:

"Ha! Hum! You have the Spring fever, Uncle Wiggily. What you need is sassafras."

"Nurse Jane has some in the bungalow," spoke Mr. Longears. "Tell her to make me some tea from that."

"No, what is needed is fresh sassafras," said Dr. Possum. "And, what is more, you must go out in the woods and dig it yourself. That will be almost as good for your Spring fever as the sassafras itself. So hop out, and dig some of the roots."

"Oh, dear!" cried Uncle Wiggily, fussy like. "I don't want to. I'd rather stay here in bed."

"But you can't!" cried Dr. Possum in his jolly voice. "Out with you!" and he pulled the bed clothes off the bunny uncle so he had to get up to keep warm.

"Well, I'll just go out and dig a little sassafras root to please him," thought Uncle Wiggily to himself, "and then I'll come back and stay in bed as long as I please. It's all nonsense thinking I have to have fresh root—the old is good enough."

"I do feel quite wretched and lazy like," said Uncle Wiggily to himself, as he limped along on his red, white and blue-striped barber-pole rheumatism crutch, that Nurse Jane had gnawed for him out of a cornstalk. "As soon as I find some sassafras I'll pull up a bit of the root and hurry back home and to bed."

Pretty soon the bunny uncle saw where some of the sassafras roots were growing, with their queer three-pointed leaves, like a mitten, with a place for your finger and thumb.

"Now to pull up the root," said the bunny uncle, as he dug down in the ground a little way with his paws, to get a better hold.

But pulling up sassafras roots is not as easy as it sounds, as you know if you have ever tried it. The roots go away down in the earth, and they are very strong.

Uncle Wiggily pulled and tugged and twisted and turned, but he could break off only little bits of the underground stalk.

"This won't do!" he said to himself. "If I don't get a big root Dr. Possum will, perhaps, send me hack for more. I'll try again."

He got his paws under a nice, big root, and he was straining his back to pull it up, when, all of a sudden, he heard a voice saying:

"How do you do?"

"Oh, hello!" exclaimed the bunny, looking up quickly, and expecting to see some friend of his, like Grandpa Goosey Gander, or Sammie Littletail, the rabbit boy. But, instead, he saw the bad old fox, who had, so many times, tried to catch the rabbit gentleman.

"Oh!" said Uncle Wiggily, astonished like. And again he said: "Oh!"

"Surprised, are you?" asked the fox, sort of curling his whiskers around his tongue, sarcastic fashion.

"A little—yes," answered Uncle Wiggily. "I didn't expect to see you."

"But I've been expecting you a long time," said the fox, grinning most impolitely. "In fact, I've been waiting for you. Just as soon as you have pulled up that sassafras root you may come with me. I'll take you off to my den, to my dear little foxes Eight, Nine and Ten. Those are their numbers. It's easier to number them than name them."

"Oh, indeed?" asked Uncle Wiggily, as politely as he could, considering everything. "And so you won't take me until I pull this sassafras root?"

"No, I'll wait until you have finished," spoke the fox. "I like you better, anyhow, flavored with sassafras. So pull away."

Uncle Wiggily tried to pull up the root, but he did not pull very hard.

"For," he thought, "as soon as I pull it up then the fox will take me, but if I don't pull it he may not."

"What's the matter? Can't you get that root up?" asked the fox, after a while. "I can't wait all day."

"Then perhaps you will kindly pull it up for me," said the bunny uncle. "I can't seem to do it."

"All right, I will," the fox said. Uncle Wiggily hopped to one side. The fox put his paws under the sassafras root. And he pulled and he pulled and he pulled, and finally, with a double extra strong pull, he pulled up the root. But it came up so suddenly, just as when you break the point off your pencil, that the fox keeled over backward in a peppersault and somersault also.

"Oh, wow!" cried the fox, as he bumped his nose. "What happened?" But Uncle Wiggily did not stay to tell. Away ran the bunny through the woods, as fast as he could go, forgetting all about his Spring fever. He was all over it.

"I thought the sassafras would cure you," said Dr. Possum, when Uncle Wiggily was safely home once more.

"The fox helped some," said the bunny uncle, with a laugh.

And if the black cat doesn't cover himself with talcum powder and make believe he's a white kid glove going to a dance, I'll tell you next about Uncle Wiggily and Jack-in-the-Pulpit.

STORY V

UNCLE WIGGILY AND THE PULPIT-JACK

"Well, how are you feeling today, Uncle Wiggily?" asked Nurse Jane Fuzzy Wuzzy, the muskrat lady housekeeper, as she saw the rabbit gentleman taking his tall silk hat down off the china closet, getting ready to go for a walk in the woods one morning.

"Why, I'm feeling pretty fine, Nurse Jane," answered the bunny uncle. "Since I ran home to get away from the fox, after he turned a peppersault from pulling too strong to get up the sassafras root, I feel much better, thank you."

"Good!" cried Nurse Jane. "Then perhaps you would not mind going to the store for me."

"Certainly not," spoke Uncle Wiggily. "What do you wish?"

"A loaf of bread," replied Miss Fuzzy Wuzzy, "also a box of matches and some sugar and crackers. But don't forget the matches whatever you do."

"I won't," promised the bunny uncle, and soon he was hopping along through the woods wondering what sort of an adventure he would have this day.

As he was going along keeping a sharp look-out for the bad fox, or the skillery-scalery alligator with the double jointed tail. Uncle Wiggily heard a voice saying:

"Oh, dear! I'll never be able to get out from under the stone and grow tall as I ought. I've pushed and pushed on it, but I can't raise it. Oh, dear; what a heavy stone!"

"Ha! Some one under a stone!" said Uncle Wiggily to himself. "That certainly is bad trouble. I wonder if I cannot help?"

The bunny uncle looked all around and down on the ground he saw a flat stone. Underneath it something green and brown was peeping out.

"Was that you who called?" asked Mr. Longears.

"It was," came the answer. "I am a Jack-in-the-Pulpit plant, you see, and I started to grow up, as all plants and flowers do when summer comes. But when I had raised my head out of the earth I found a big stone over me, and now I can grow no more. I've pushed and pushed until my back aches, and I can't lift the stone."

"I'll do it for you," said Uncle Wiggily kindly, and he did, taking it off the Pulpit-Jack.

Then the Jack began growing up, and he had been held down so long that he grew quite quickly, so that even while Uncle Wiggily was watching, the Jack and his pulpit were almost regular size.

A Jack-in-the-Pulpit, you know, is a queer flower that grows in our woods. Sometimes it is called an Indian turnip, but don't eat it, for it is very biting. The Jack is a tall green chap, who stands in the middle of his pulpit, which is like a little pitcher, with a curved top to it. A pulpit, you know, is where some one preaches on Sunday.

"Thank you very much for lifting the stone off me so I could grow," said the Jack to Uncle Wiggily. "If ever I can do you a favor I will."

"Oh, pray don't mention it," replied the rabbit gentleman, with a low bow. "It was a mere pleasure, I assure you."

Then the rabbit gentleman hopped on to the store, to get the matches, the crackers, the bread and other things for Nurse Jane.

"And I must be sure not to forget the matches," Uncle Wiggily said to himself. "If I did Nurse Jane could not make a fire to cook supper."

There was an April shower while Uncle Wiggily was in the store, and he waited for the rain to stop falling before he started back to his hollow stump bungalow. Then the sun came out very hot and strong and shone down through the wet leaves of the trees in the woods.

Along hopped the bunny uncle, and he was wondering what he would have for supper that night.

"I hope it's something good," he said, "to make up for not having an adventure."

"Don't you call that an adventure—lifting the stone off the Jack-in-the-Pulpit so he could grow?" asked a bird, sitting up in a tree.

"Well, that was a little adventure." said Uncle Wiggily. "But I want one more exciting; a big one."

And he is going to have one in about a minute. Just you wait and you'll hear all about it.

The sun was shining hotter and hotter, and Uncle Wiggily was thinking that it was about time to get out his extra-thin fur coat when, all of a sudden, he felt something very hot behind him.

"Why, that sun is really burning!" cried the bunny. Then he heard a little ant boy, who was crawling on the ground, cry out:

"Fire! Fire! Fire! Uncle Wiggily's bundle of groceries is on fire! Fire! Fire!"

"Oh, my!" cried the bunny uncle, as he felt hotter and hotter, "The sun must have set fire to the box of matches. Oh, what shall I do?" He dropped his bundle of groceries, and looking around at them he saw, surely enough, the matches were on fire. They were all blazing.

"Call the fire department! Get out the water bugs!" cried the little ant boy. "Fire! Water! Water! Fire!"

"That's what I want—water," cried the bunny uncle. "Oh, if I could find a spring of water. I could put the blazing matches, save some of them, perhaps, and surely save the bread and crackers. Oh, for some water!"

Uncle Wiggily and the ant boy ran here and there in the woods looking for a spring of water. But they could find none, and the bread and crackers were just beginning to burn when a voice cried:

"Here is water, Uncle Wiggily!"

"Where? Where?" asked the rabbit gentleman, all excited like. "Where?"

"Inside my pulpit," was the answer, and Uncle Wiggily saw, not far away, the Jack-plant he had helped from under the stone.

"When it rained a while ago, my pitcher-pulpit became filled with water," went on Jack. "If you will just tip me over, sideways, I'll splash the water on the blazing matches and put them out."

"I'll do it!" cried Uncle Wiggily, and he quickly did. The pulpit held water as good as a milk pitcher could, and when the water splashed on the fire that fire gave one hiss, like a goose, and went out.

"Oh, you certainly did me a favor, Mr. Pulpit-Jack," said Uncle Wiggily. "Though the matches are burned, the bread and crackers are saved, and I can get more matches." Which he did, so Nurse Jane could make a fire in the stove.

So you see Uncle Wiggily had an adventure after all, and quite an exciting one, too, and if the lemon drop doesn't fall on the stick of peppermint candy and make it sneeze when it goes to the moving pictures, I'll tell you next about Uncle Wiggily and the violets.

STORY VI

UNCLE WIGGILY AND THE VIOLETS

Down in the kitchen of the hollow stump bungalow there was a great clattering of pots and pans. Uncle Wiggily Longears, the rabbit gentleman who lived in the bungalow, sat up in bed, having been awakened by the noise, and he said:

"Well, I wonder what Nurse Jane Fuzzy Wuzzy is doing now? She certainly is busy at something, and it can't be making the breakfast buckwheat cakes, either, for she has stopped baking them."

"I say, Miss Fuzzy Wuzzy, what's going on down in your kitchen?" called the rabbit gentleman out loud.

"I'm washing," answered the muskrat lady.

"Washing what; the dishes?" the bunny uncle wanted to know. "If you wash them as hard as it sounds, there won't be any of them left for dinner, and I haven't had my breakfast yet."

"No, I'm getting ready to wash the clothes, and I wish you'd come down and eat, so I can clear away the table things!" called the muskrat lady.

"Oh, dear! Clothes-washing!" cried Uncle Wiggily, making his pink nose twinkle in a funny way. "I don't like to be around the bungalow when that is being done. I guess I'll get my breakfast and go for a walk. Clothes have to be washed, I suppose," went on the rabbit gentleman, "and when Nurse Jane has been ill I have washed them myself, but I do not like it. I'll go off in the woods."

And so, having had his breakfast of carrot pudding, with turnip sauce sprinkled over the top, Uncle Wiggily took his red, white and blue striped rheumatism crutch, and hopped along.

The woods were getting more and more beautiful every day as the weather grew warmer. The leaves on the trees were larger, and here and there, down in the green moss, that was like a carpet on the ground, could be seen wild flowers growing up.

"I wonder what sort of an adventure I will have today?" thought the bunny uncle as he went on and on. "A nice one, I hope."

And, as he said this, Uncle Wiggily heard some voices speaking.

"Oh, dear!" exclaimed a sad little voice, "no one will ever see us here! Of what use are we in the world? We are so small that we cannot be noticed. We are not brightly colored, like the red rose, and all that will happen to us will be that a cow will come along and eat us, or step on us with her big foot."

"Hush! You musn't talk that way," said another voice. "You were put here to grow, and do the best you know how. Don't be finding fault."

"I wonder who can be talking?" said Uncle Wiggily. "I must look around." So he looked up in the air, but though he heard the leaves whispering he knew they had not spoken. Then he looked to the right, to the left, in front and behind, but he saw no one. Then he looked down, and right at his feet was a clump of blue violet flowers.

"Did you speak?" asked Uncle Wiggily of the violets.

"Yes," answered one who had been finding fault. "I was telling my sisters and brothers that we are of no use in the world. We just grow up here in the woods, where no one sees us, and we never can have any fun. I want to be a big, red rose and grow in a garden."

"Oh, my!" cried Uncle Wiggily. "I never heard of a violet turning into a rose." Then the mother violet spoke and said:

"I tell my little girl-flower that she ought to be happy to grow here in the nice woods, in the green moss, where it is so cool and moist. But she does not seem to be happy, nor are some of the other violets."

"Well, that isn't right," Uncle Wiggily said, kindly. "I am sure you violets can do some good in this world. You are pretty to look at, and nice to smell, and that is more than can be said of some things."

"Oh, I want to do something big!" said the fault-finding violet. "I want to go out in the world and see things."

"So do I! And I! And I!" cried other violets.

Uncle Wiggily thought for a minute, and then he said:

"I'll do this. I'll dig up a bunch of you violets, who want a change, and take you with me for a walk. I will leave some earth on your roots so you won't die, and we shall see what happens."

"Oh, goodie!" cried the violets. So Uncle Wiggily dug them up with his paws, putting some cool moss around their roots, and when they had said good-by to the mother violet away they went traveling with the bunny uncle.

"Oh, this is fine!" cried the first violet, nodding her head in the breeze. "It is very kind of you, Uncle Wiggily to take us with you. I wish we could do you a kindness."

And then a bad old fox jumped out from behind a stump, and started to grab the rabbit gentleman. But when the fox saw the pretty violets and smelled their sweetness, the fox felt sorry at having been bad and said:

"Excuse me, Uncle Wiggily. I'm sorry I tried to bite you. The sight of those pretty violets makes me feel happier than I did. I am going to try to be good."

"I am glad of it," said Mr. Longears, as he hopped on through the woods. "You see, you have already done some good in this world, even if you are only tiny flowers," he said to the violets.

Then Uncle Wiggily went on to his hollow stump bungalow, and, reaching there, he heard Nurse Jane saying:

"Oh, dear! This is terrible. Here I have the clothes almost washed, and not a bit of bluing to rinse them in. Oh, why didn't I tell Wiggy to bring me some blueing from the store? Oh, dear!"

"Ha! Perhaps these will do to make blue water," said the bunny uncle, holding out the bunch of violets. "Would you like to help Nurse Jane?" he asked the flowers.

"Oh, yes, very much!" cried the violets.

Then Uncle Wiggily dipped their blue heads in the clean rinsing water—just a little dip so as not to make them catch cold—and enough color came out of the violets to make the water properly blue for Nurse Jane's clothes, so she could finish the washing.

"So you see you have done more good in the world," said Uncle Wiggily to the flowers. Then he took them back and planted them in the woods where they lived, and very glad they were to return, too.

"We have seen enough of the world," they said, and thereafter they were glad enough to live down in the moss with the mother violet. And if the umbrella doesn't turn inside out so the handle tickles its ribs and makes it laugh in school, I'll tell you next about Uncle Wiggily and the high tree.

STORY VII

UNCLE WIGGILY AND THE HIGH TREE

Uncle Wiggily Longears, the nice rabbit gentleman, stood in front of the looking glass trying on a new tall silk hat he had just bought ready for Easter Sunday, which would happen in about a week or two.

"Do you think it looks well on me, Nurse Jane?" asked the bunny uncle, of the muskrat lady housekeeper, who came in from the kitchen of the hollow stump bungalow, having just finished washing the dishes.

"Why, yes, I think your new hat is very nice," she said.

"Do you think I ought to have the holes for my ears cut a little larger?" asked the bunny uncle. "I mean the holes cut, not my ears."

"Well, just a little larger wouldn't hurt any," replied Miss Fuzzy Wuzzy. "I'll cut them for you," and she did, with her scissors. For Uncle Wiggily had to wear his tall silk hat with his ears sticking up through holes cut in it. His ears were too large to go under the hat, and he could not very well fold them down.

"There, now I guess I'm all right to go for a walk in the woods," said the rabbit gentleman, taking another look at himself in the glass. It was not a proud look, you understand. Uncle Wiggily just wanted to look right and proper, and he wasn't at all stuck up, even if his ears were, but he couldn't help that.

So off he started, wondering what sort of an adventure he would have that day. He passed the place where the blue violets were growing in the green moss—the same violets he had used to make Nurse Jane's blueing water for her clothes the other day, as I told you. And the violets were glad to see the bunny uncle.

Then Uncle Wiggily met Grandfather Goosey Gander, the nice old goose gentleman, and the two friends walked on together, talking about how much cornmeal you could buy with a lollypop, and all about the best way to eat fried ice cream carrots.

"That's a very nice hat you have on, Uncle Wiggily," said Grandpa Goosey, after a bit.

"Glad you like it," answered the bunny uncle. "It's for Easter."

"I think I'll get one for myself," went on Mr. Gander. "Do you think I would look well in it?"

"Try on mine and see," offered Uncle Wiggily most kindly. So he took his new, tall silk hat off his head, pulling his ears out of the holes Nurse Jane had cut for them, and handed it to Grandfather Goosey Gander—handed the hat, I mean, not his ears, though of course the holes went with the hat.

"There, how do I look?" asked the goose gentleman.

"Quite stylish and proper," replied Mr. Longears.

"I'd like to see myself before I buy a hat like this," went on Grandpa Goosey. "I hope it doesn't make me look too tall."

"Here's a spring of water over by this old stump," spoke Uncle Wiggily. "You can see yourself in that, for it is just like a looking glass."

Grandpa Goosey leaned over to see how Uncle Wiggily's tall, silk hat looked, when, all of a sudden, along came a puff of wind, caught the hat under the brim, and as Grandpa Goosey had no ears to hold it on his head (as the bunny uncle had) away sailed the hat up in the air, and it landed right in the top of a big, high tree.

"Oh, dear!" cried Uncle Wiggily.

"Oh, dear!" said Grandpa Goosey. "I'm very sorry that happened. Oh, dear!"

"It wasn't your fault at all," spoke Uncle Wiggily kindly. "It was the wind."

"But with your nice, new tall silk hat up in that high tree, how are we ever going to get it down," asked the goose gentleman.

"I don't know," answered Uncle Wiggily. "Let me think."

So he thought for a minute or two, and then he said:

"There are three ways by which we may get the hat down. One is to ask the wind to blow it back to us, another is to climb up the tree and get the hat ourselves, and the third is to ask the tree to shake it down to us. We'll try the wind first."

So Uncle Wiggily and Grandpa Goosey asked the wind that had blown the hat up in the top of the high tree to kindly blow it back again. But the wind had gone far out to sea, and would not be back for a week. So that way of getting the hat was of no use.

"Mr. High Tree, will you kindly shake my hat down to me?" begged Uncle Wiggily next.

"I would like to, very much," the tree answered politely, "but I cannot shake when there is no wind to blow me. We trees cannot shake ourselves, you know. We can only shake when the wind blows us, and until the wind comes back I cannot shake."

"Too bad!" said Uncle Wiggily. "Then the only way left for us to do, Grandpa Goosey, is to climb the tree."

But this was easier said than done, for neither a rabbit nor a goose gentleman is made for climbing up trees, though when he was a young chap Grandpa Goosey had flown up into little trees, and Uncle Wiggily had jumped over them. But that was long, long ago.

Try as they did, neither the rabbit gentleman nor the goose gentleman could climb up after the tall silk hat.

"What are we going to do?" asked Grandpa Goosey.

"I don't know," replied Mr. Longears. "I guess I'll have to go get Billie or Johnnie Bushytail, the squirrel boys, to climb the tree for us. Yes, that's what I'll do; and then I can get my hat."

Uncle Wiggily started off through the woods to look for one of the Bushytail chaps, while Grandpa Goosey stayed near the tree, to catch the hat in case it should happen to fall by itself.

All of a sudden Uncle Wiggily heard some one coming along whistling, and then he heard a loud pounding sound, and next he saw Toodle Flat-tail, the beaver boy, walking in the woods.

"Oh, Toodle! You're the very one I want!" cried Uncle Wiggily. "My hat is in a high tree and I can't get it. With your strong teeth, just made for cutting down trees, will you kindly cut down this one, and get my hat for me?"

"I will," said the little beaver chap. But when he began to gnaw the tree, to make it fall, the tree cried:

"Oh, Mr. Wind, please come and blow on me so I can shake Uncle Wiggily's hat to him, and then I won't have to be gnawed down. Please blow, Mr. Wind."

So the wind hurried back and blew the tree this way and that. Down toppled Uncle Wiggily's hat, not in the least hurt, and so everything was all right again, and Uncle Wiggily and Grandpa Goosey and Toodle Flat-tail were happy. And the tree was extra glad as it did not have to be gnawed down.

Down toppled Uncle Wiggily's hat, not in the least hurt.

And if the little mouse doesn't go to sleep in the cat's cradle and scare poor pussy so her tail swells up like a balloon, I'll tell you next about Uncle Wiggily and the peppermint.

STORY VIII

UNCLE WIGGILY AND THE PEPPERMINT

"Uncle Wiggily, would you mind going to the store for me?" asked Nurse Jane Fuzzy Wuzzy, the muskrat lady housekeeper, one morning, as she came in from the kitchen of the hollow stump bungalow, where she had been getting ready the breakfast for the rabbit gentleman.

"Go to the store? Why of course I'll go, Miss Fuzzy Wuzzy," answered the bunny uncle. "Which store?"

"The drug store."

"The drug store? What do you want; talcum powder or court plaster?"

"Neither one," answered Nurse Jane. "I want some peppermint."

"Peppermint candy?" Uncle Wiggily wanted to know.

"Not exactly," went on Nurse Jane. "But I want a little of the peppermint juice with which some kind of candy is flavored. I want to take some peppermint juice myself, for I have indigestion. Dr. Possum says peppermint is good for it. I must have eaten a little too much cheese pudding last night."

"I'll get you the peppermint with pleasure," said the bunny uncle, starting off with his tall silk hat and his red, white and blue striped rheumatism barber pole crutch.

"Better get it in a bottle," spoke Nurse Jane, with a laugh. "You can't carry peppermint in your pocket, unless it's peppermint candy, and I don't want that kind."

"All right," Uncle Wiggily said, and then, with the bottle, which Nurse Jane gave him, he hopped on, over the fields and through the woods to the drug store.

But when he got there the cupboard was bare—. No! I mustn't say that. It doesn't belong here. I mean when Uncle Wiggily reached the drug store it was closed, and there was a sign in the door which said the monkey-doodle gentleman who kept the drug store had gone to a baseball-moving-picture show, and wouldn't be back for a long while.

"Then I wonder where I am going to get Nurse Jane's peppermint?" asked Uncle Wiggily of himself. "I'd better go see if Dr. Possum has any."

But while Uncle Wiggily was going on through the woods once more, he gave a sniff and a whiff, and, all of a sudden, he smelled a peppermint smell.

The rabbit gentleman stood still, looking around and making his pink nose twinkle like a pair of roller skates. While he was doing this along came a cow lady chewing some grass for her complexion.

"What are you doing here, Uncle Wiggily?" asked the cow lady.

Uncle Wiggily told her how he had gone to the drug store for peppermint for Nurse Jane, and how he had found the store closed, so he could not get any.

"But I smell peppermint here in the woods," went on the bunny uncle. "Can it be that the drug store monkey doodle has left some here for me?"

"No, what you smell is—that," said the cow lady, pointing her horns toward some green plants growing near a little babbling brook of water. The plants had dark red stems that were square instead of round.

"It does smell like peppermint," said Uncle Wiggily, going closer and sniffing and snuffing.

"It is peppermint," said the cow lady. "That is the peppermint plant you see."

"Oh, now I remember," Uncle Wiggily exclaimed. "They squeeze the juice out of the leaves, and that's peppermint flavor for candy or for indigestion."

"Exactly," spoke the cow lady, "and I'll help you squeeze out some of this juice in the bottle for Nurse Jane."

Then Uncle Wiggily and the cow lady pulled up some of the peppermint plants and squeezed out the juice between two clean, flat stones, the cow lady stepping on them while Uncle Wiggily caught the juice in the empty bottle as it ran out.

"My! But that is strong!" cried the bunny uncle, as he smelled of the bottle of peppermint. It was so sharp that it made tears come into his eyes. "I should think that would cure indigestion and everything else," he said to the cow lady.

"Tell Nurse Jane to take only a little of it in sweet water," said the cow lady. "It is very strong. So be careful of it."

"I will," promised Uncle Wiggily. "And thank you for getting the peppermint for me. I don't know what I would have done without you, as the drug store was closed."

Then he hopped on through the woods to the hollow stump bungalow. He had not quite reached it when, all of a sudden, there was a rustling in the hushes, and out from behind a bramble bush jumped a big black bear. Not a nice good bear, like Neddie or Beckie Stubtail, but a bear who cried:

"Ah, ha! Oh, ho! Here is some one whom I can bite and scratch! A nice tender rabbit chap! Ah, ha! Oh, ho!"

"Are—are you going to scratch and bite me?" asked Uncle Wiggily.

"I am," said the bear, snappish like. "Get ready. Here I come!" and he started toward Uncle Wiggily, who was so frightened that he could not hop away.

"I'm going to hug you, too," said the bear. Bears always hug, you know.

"Well, this is, indeed, a sorry day for me," said Uncle Wiggily, sadly. "Still, if you are going to hug, bite and scratch me, I suppose it can't be helped."

"Not the least in the world can it be helped," said the bear, cross-like and unpleasant. "So don't try!"

"Well, if you are going to hug me I had better take this bottle out of my pocket, so when you squeeze me the glass won't break," Uncle Wiggily said. "Here, when you are through being so mean to me perhaps you will be good enough to take this to Nurse Jane for her indigestion, but don't hug her."

"I won't," promised the bear, taking the bottle which Uncle Wiggily handed him. "What's in it?"

Before Uncle Wiggily could answer, the bear opened the bottle, and, seeing something in it, cried:

"I guess I'll taste this. Maybe it's good to eat." Down his big, red throat he poured the strong peppermint juice, and then—well, I guess you know what happened.

"Oh, wow! Oh, me! Oh, my! Wow! Ouch! Ouchie! Itchie!" roared the bear. "My throat is on fire! I must have some water!" And, dropping the bottle, away he ran to the spring, leaving Uncle Wiggily safe, and not hurt a bit.

Then the rabbit gentleman hurried back and squeezed out more peppermint juice for Nurse Jane, whose indigestion was soon cured. And as for the bear, he had a sore throat for a week and a day.

So this teaches us that peppermint is good for scaring bears, as well as for putting in candy. And if the snow man doesn't come in our house and sit by the gas stove until he melts into a puddle of molasses, I'll tell you next about Uncle Wiggily and the birch tree.

STORY IX

UNCLE WIGGILY AND THE BIRCH TREE

Uncle Wiggily Longears, the nice old rabbit gentleman, was walking along through the woods one afternoon, when he came to the hollow stump school, where the lady mouse teacher taught the animal boys and girls how to jump, crack nuts, dig homes under ground, and do all manner of things that animal folk have to do.

And just as the rabbit gentleman was wondering whether or not school was out, he heard a voice inside the hollow stump, saying:

"Oh, dear! I wish I had some one to help me. I'll never get them clean all by myself. Oh, dear!"

"Ha! That sounds like trouble!" thought Mr. Longears to himself. "I wonder who it is, and if I can help? I guess I'd better see."

He looked in through a window, and there he saw the lady mouse teacher cleaning off the school black-boards. The boards were all covered with white chalk marks, you see.

"What's the matter, lady mouse teacher?" asked Uncle Wiggily, making a polite, low bow.

"Oh, I told Johnnie and Billy Bushytail, the two squirrel boys, to stay in and clean off the black-boards, so they would be all ready for tomorrow's lesson," said the lady mouse. "But they forgot, and ran off to play ball with Jackie and Peetie Bow Wow, the puppy dog boys. So I have to clean the boards myself. And I really ought to be home now, for I am very tired."

"Then you trot right along," said Uncle Wiggily, kindly. "Tie a knot in your tail, so you won't step on it, and hurry along."

"But what about the black-boards?" asked the lady mouse. "They must be cleaned off."

"I'll attend to that," promised the bunny uncle. "I will clean them myself. Run along, Miss Mouse."

So Miss Mouse thanked the bunny uncle, and ran along, and the rabbit gentleman began brushing the chalk marks off the black-boards, at the same time humming a little tune that went this way:

> "I'd love to be a teacher,
> Within a hollow stump.
> I'd teach the children how to fall,
> And never get a bump.
>
> I'd let them out at recess,
> A game of tag to play;
> I'd give them all fresh lollypops
> 'Most every other day!"

"Oh, my! Wouldn't we just love to come to school to you!" cried a voice at the window, and, looking up. Uncle Wiggily saw Billie Bushytail, the boy squirrel, and brother Johnnie with him.

"Ha! What happened you two chaps?" asked the bunny uncle. "Why did you run off without cleaning the black-boards for the lady mouse teacher?"

"We forgot," said Johnnie, sort of ashamed-like and sorry. "That's what we came back to do—clean the boards."

"Well, that was good of you," spoke Uncle Wiggily. "But I have the boards nearly cleaned now."

"Then we will give them a dusting with our tails, and that will finish them," said Billie, and the squirrel boys did, so the black-boards were very clean.

"Now it's time to go home," said Uncle Wiggily. So he locked the school, putting the key under the doormat, where the lady mouse could find it in the morning, and, with the Bushytail squirrel boys, he started off through the woods.

"You and Billie can go back to your play, now, Johnnie," said the bunny uncle. "It was good of you to leave it to come back to do what you were told."

The three animal friends hopped and scrambled on together, until, all of a sudden, the bad old fox, who so often had made trouble for Uncle Wiggily, jumped out from behind a bush, crying:

"Ah, ha! Now I have you, Mr. Longears—and two squirrels besides. Good luck!"

"Bad luck!" whispered Billie.

The fox made a grab for the rabbit gentleman, but, all of a sudden, the paw of the bad creature slipped in some mud and down he went, head first, into a puddle of water, coughing and sneezing.

"Come on, Uncle Wiggily!" quickly cried Billie and Johnnie. "This is our chance. We'll run away before the fox gets the water out of his eyes. He can't see us now."

So away ran the rabbit gentleman and the squirrel boys, but soon the fox had dried his eyes on his big brush of a tail, and on he came after them.

"Oh, I'll get you! I'll get you!" he cried, running very fast. But Uncle Wiggily and Billie and Johnnie ran fast, too. The fox was coming closer, however, and Billie, looking back, said:

"Oh, I know what let's do, Uncle Wiggily. Let's take the path that leads over the duck pond ocean. That's shorter, and we can get to your bungalow before the fox can catch us. He won't dare come across the bridge over the duck pond, for Old Dog Percival will come out and bite him if he does."

"Very well," said Uncle Wiggily, "over the bridge we will go."

But alas! Also sorrowfulness and sadness! When the three friends got to the bridge it wasn't there. The wind had blown the bridge down, and there was no way of getting across the duck pond ocean, for neither Uncle Wiggily nor the squirrel boys could swim very well.

"Oh, what are we going to do?" cried Billie, sadly.

"We must get across somehow!" chattered Johnnie, "for here comes the fox!"

And, surely enough the fox was coming, having by this time gotten all the water out of his eyes, so he could see very well.

"Oh, if we only had a boat!" exclaimed Uncle Wiggily, looking along the shore of the pond, but there was no boat to be seen.

Nearer and nearer came the fox! Uncle Wiggily and the squirrel boys were just going to jump in the water, whether or not they could swim, when, all at once, a big white birch tree on the edge of the woods near the pond, said:

"Listen, Uncle Wiggily and I will save you. Strip off some of my bark. It will not hurt me, and you can make a little canoe boat of it, as the Indians used to do. Then, in the birch bark boat you can sail across the water and the fox can't get you."

"Good! Thank you!" cried the bunny uncle. With their sharp teeth he, Billie and Johnnie peeled off long strips of birch bark. They quickly bent them in the shape of a boat and sewed up the ends with long thorns for needles and ribbon grass for thread.

"Quick! Into the birch bark boat!" cried Uncle Wiggily, and they all jumped in, just as the fox came along. Billie and Johnnie held up their bushy tails, and Uncle Wiggily held up his tall silk hat for sails, and soon they were safe on the other shore and the fox, not being able to swim, could not get them.

So that's how the birch tree of the woods saved the bunny uncle and the squirrels, for which, I am very glad, as I want to write more stories about them. And if the gold fish doesn't tickle the wax doll's nose with his tail when she looks in the tank to see what he has for breakfast, I'll tell you next about Uncle Wiggily and the butternut tree.

STORY X

UNCLE WIGGILY AND THE BUTTERNUT TREE

"Well, I declare!" exclaimed Nurse Jane Fuzzy Wuzzy, the muskrat lady housekeeper of Uncle Wiggily Longears, the rabbit, as she looked in the pantry of the hollow stump bungalow one day. "Well, I do declare!"

"What's the matter?" asked Mr. Longears, peeping over the top of his spectacles. "I hope that the chimney hasn't fallen down, or the egg beater run away with the potato masher."

"No, nothing like that," Nurse Jane said. "But we haven't any butter!"

"No butter?" spoke Uncle Wiggily, sort of puzzled like, and abstracted.

"Not a bit of butter for supper," went on Nurse Jane, sadly.

"Ha! That sounds like something from Mother Goose. Not a bit of butter for supper," laughed Uncle Wiggily. "Not a bit of batter-butter for the pitter-patter supper. If Peter Piper picked a pit of peckled pippers—"

"Oh, don't start that!" begged Nurse Jane. "All I need is some supper for butter—no some bupper for batter—oh, dear! I'll never get it straight!" she cried.

"I'll say it for you," said Uncle Wiggily, kindly. "I know what you want—some butter for supper. I'll go get it for you."

"Thank you," Nurse Jane exclaimed, and so the old rabbit gentleman started off over the fields and through the woods for the butter store.

The monkey-doodle gentleman waited on him, and soon Uncle Wiggily was on his way back to the hollow stump bungalow with the butter for supper, and he was thinking how nice the carrot muffins would taste, for Nurse Jane had promised to make some, and Uncle Wiggily was sort of smacking his whiskers and twinkling his nose, when, all at once, he heard some one in the woods calling:

"Uncle Wiggily! Oh, I say, Uncle Wiggily! Can't you stop for a moment and say how-d'-do?"

"Why, of course, I can," answered the bunny, and, looking around the corner of an old log, he saw Grandpa Whackum, the old beaver gentleman, who lived with Toodle and Noodle Flat-tail, the beaver boys.

"Come in and sit down for a minute and rest yourself," invited Grandpa Whackum.

"I will," said Uncle Wiggily. "And I'll leave my butter outside where it will be cool," for Grandpa Whackum lived down in an underground house, where it was so warm, in summer, that butter would melt.

Grandpa Whackum was a beaver, and he was called Whackum because he used to whack his broad, flat tail on the ground, like beating a drum, to warn the other beavers of danger. Beavers, you know, are something like big muskrats, and they like water. Their tails are flat, like a pancake or egg turner.

"Well, how are things with you, and how is Nurse Jane?" asked Grandpa Whackum.

"Oh, everything is fine," said Uncle Wiggily. "Nurse Jane is well. I've just been to the store to get her some butter."

"That's just like you; always doing something for some one," said Grandpa Whackum, pleased like.

Then the two friends talked for some little while longer, until it was almost 6 o'clock, and time for Uncle Wiggily to go.

"I'll take my butter and travel along," he said. But when he went outside, where he had left the pound of butter on a flat stump, it wasn't there.

"Why, this is queer," said the bunny uncle. "I wonder if Nurse Jane could have come along and taken it to the hollow stump bungalow herself?"

"More likely a bad fox took the butter," spoke the old gentleman beaver. "But we can soon tell. I'll look in the dirt around the stump and see whose footprints are there. A fox makes different tracks from a muskrat."

So Grandpa Whackum looked and he said:

"Why, this is queer. I can only see beaver tracks and rabbit tracks near the stump. Only you and I were here and we didn't take anything."

"But where is my butter?" asked Uncle Wiggily.

Just then, off in the woods, near the beaver house, came the sound of laughter and voices cailed:

"Oh, it's my turn now, Toodle."

"Yes, Noodle, and then it's mine. Oh, what fun we are having, aren't we?"

"It's Toodle and Noodle—my two beaver grandsons," said Grandpa Whackum. "I wonder if they could have taken your butter? Come; we'll find out."

They went softly over behind a clump of bushes and there they saw Toodle and Noodle sliding down the slanting log of a tree, that was like a little hill, only there was no snow on it.

"Why, they're coasting!" cried Grandpa Whackum. "And how they can do it without snow I don't see."

"But I see!" said Uncle Wiggily. "Those two little beaver boys have taken my butter that I left outside of your house and with the butter they have greased the slanting log until it is slippery as ice. That's how they slide down—on Nurse Jane's butter."

"Oh, the little rascals!" cried Grandpa Whackum.

"Well, they didn't mean anything wrong," Uncle Wiggily kindly said. Then he called; "Toodle! Noodle! Is any of my butter left?"

"Your butter?" cried Noodle, surprised like.

"Was that your butter?" asked Toodle. "Oh, please forgive us! We thought no one wanted it, and we took it to grease the log so we could slide down. It was as good as sliding down a muddy, slippery bank of mud into the lake."

"We used all your butter," spoke Noodle. "Every bit."

"Oh, dear! That's too bad!" Uncle Wiggily said. "It is now after 6 o'clock and all the stores will be closed. How can I get more?" And he looked at the butter the beaver boys had spread on the tree. It could not be used for bread, as it was all full of bark.

"Oh, how can I get some good butter for Nurse Jane?" asked the bunny uncle sadly.

"Ha! I will give you some," spoke a voice high in the air.

"Who are you?" asked Uncle Wiggily, startled.

"I am the butternut tree," was the answer. "I'll drop some nuts down and all you will have to do will be to crack them, pick out the meats and squeeze out the butter. It is almost as good as that which you buy in the store."

"Good!" cried Uncle Wiggily, "and thank you."

Then the butter tree rattled down some butternuts, which Uncle Wiggily took home, and Nurse Jane said the butter squeezed from them was very good. And Toodle and Noodle were sorry for having taken Uncle Wiggily's other butter to make a slippery tree slide, but they meant no harm.

So if the pussy cat doesn't take the lollypop stick to make a mud pie, and not give any ice cream cones to the rag doll, I'll tell you next about Uncle Wiggily and Lulu's hat.

STORY XI

UNCLE WIGGILY AND LULU'S HAT

"Uncle Wiggily, do you want to do something for me?" asked Nurse Jane Fuzzy Wuzzy, the muskrat lady housekeeper, of the rabbit gentleman one day as he started out from his hollow stump bungalow to take a walk in the woods.

"Do something for you, Nurse Jane? Why, of course, I want to," spoke Mr. Longears. "What is it?"

"Just take this piece of pie over to Mrs. Wibblewobble, the duck lady," went on Miss Fuzzy Wuzzy. "I promised to let her taste how I made apple pie out of cabbage leaves."

"And very cleverly you do it, too," said Uncle Wiggily, with a polite bow. "I know, for I have eaten some myself. I will gladly take this pie to Mrs. Wibblewobble," and off through the woods Uncle Wiggily started with it.

He soon reached the duck lady's house, and Mrs. Wibblewobble was very glad indeed to get the piece of Nurse Jane's pie.

"I'll save a bit for Lulu and Alice, my two little duck girls," said Mrs. Wibblewobble.

"Why, aren't they home?" asked Uncle Wiggily.

"No, Lulu has gone over to a little afternoon party which Nannie Wagtail, the goat girl, is having, and Alice has gone to see Grandfather Goosey Gander. Jiminie is off playing ball with Jackie and Peetie Bow Wow, the puppy dog boys, so I am home alone."

"I hope you are not lonesome," said Uncle Wiggily.

"Oh, no, thank you," answered the duck lady. "I have too much to do. Thank Nurse Jane for her pie."

"I shall," Uncle Wiggily promised, as he started off through the woods again. He had not gone far before, all of a sudden, he did not stoop low enough as he was hopping under a tree and, the first thing he knew, his tall silk hat was knocked off his head and into a puddle of water.

"Oh, dear!" cried Uncle Wiggily, as he picked up his hat. "I shall never be able to wear it again until it is cleaned and ironed. And how I can have that done out here in the woods is more than I know."

"Ah, but I know," said a voice in a tree overhead.

"Who are you, and what do you know?" asked the bunny uncle, surprised like and hopeful.

"I know where you can have your silk hat cleaned and ironed smooth," said the voice. "I am the tailor bird, and I do those things. Let me have your hat, Uncle Wiggily, and I'll fix it for you."

Down flew the kind bird, and Uncle Wiggily gave him the hat.

"But what shall I wear while I'm waiting?" asked the bunny uncle. "It is too soon for me to be going about without my hat. I'll need something on my head while you are fixing my silk stovepipe, dear Tailor Bird."

"Oh, that is easy," said the bird. "Just pick some of those thick, green leafy ferns and make yourself a hat of them."

"The very thing!" cried Uncle Wiggily. Then he fastened some woodland ferns together and easily made himself a hat that would keep off the sun, if it would not keep off the rain. But then it wasn't raining.

"There you are, Uncle Wiggily!" called the tailor bird at last. "Your silk hat is ready to wear again."

"Thank you," spoke the bunny uncle, as he laid aside the ferns, also thanking them. "Now I am like myself again," and he hopped on through the woods, wondering whether or not he was to have any more adventures that day.

Mr. Longears had not gone on very much farther before he heard a rustling in the bushes, and then a sad little voice said:

"Oh, dear! How sad! I don't believe I'll go to the party now! All the others would make fun of me! Oh, dear! Oh, dear!"

"Ha! That sounds like trouble!" said the bunny uncle. "I must see what it means."

He looked through the bushes and there, sitting on a log, he saw Lulu Wibblewobble, the little duck girl, who was crying very hard, the tears rolling down her yellow bill.

"Why, Lulu! What's the matter?" asked Uncle Wiggily.

"Oh, dear!" answered the little quack-quack child. "I can't go to the party; that's what's the matter."

"Why can't you go?" Uncle Wiggily wanted to know. "I saw your mother a little while ago, and she said you were going."

"I know I was going," spoke Lulu, "but I'm not now, for the wind blew my nice new hat into the puddle of muddy water, and now look at it!" and she held up a very much beraggled and debraggled hat of lace and straw and ribbons and flowers.

"Oh, dear! That hat is in a bad state, to be sure," said Uncle Wiggily. "But don't cry, Lulu. Almost the same thing happened to me and the tailor bird made my hat as good as ever. Mine was all mud, too, like yours. Come, I'll take you to the tailor bird."

"You are very kind, Uncle Wiggily," spoke Lulu, "but if I go there I may not get back in time for the party, and I want to wear my new hat to it, very much."

"Ha! I see!" cried the bunny uncle. "You want to look nice at the party. Well, that's right, of course. And I don't believe the tailor bird could clean your hat in time, for it is so fancy he would have to be very careful of it.

"But you can do as I did, make a hat out of ferns, and wear that to Nannie Wagtail's party. I'll help you."

"Oh, how kind you are!" cried the little duck girl.

So she went along with Uncle Wiggily to where the ferns grew in the wood, leaving her regular hat at the tailor bird's nest to be cleaned and pressed.

Uncle Wiggily made Lulu the cutest hat out of fern leaves. Oh, I wish you could have seen it. There wasn't one like it even in the five and ten-cent store.

"Wear that to Nannie's party, Lulu," said the rabbit gentleman, and Lulu did, the hat being fastened to her feathers with a long pin made from the stem of a fern. And when Lulu reached the party all the animal girls cried out:

"Oh, what a sweet, lovely, cute, dear, cunning, swell and stylish hat! Where did you get it?"

"Uncle Wiggily made it," answered Lulu, and all the girls said they were going to get one just like it. And they did, so that fern hats became very fashionable and stylish in Woodland, and Lulu had a fine time at the party.

So this teaches us that even a mud puddle is of some use, and if the rubber plant doesn't stretch too far, and tickle the gold fish under the chin making it sneeze, the next story will be about Uncle Wiggily and the snow drops.

STORY XII

UNCLE WIGGILY AND THE SNOW DROPS

"Uncle Wiggily! Uncle Wiggily! Will you come with me?" called a voice under the window of the hollow stump bungalow, where the old gentleman rabbit was sitting, half asleep, one nice, warm afternoon.

"Ha! Come with you? Who is it wants me to come with them?" asked the bunny gentleman. "I hope it isn't the bad fox, or the skillery-scalery alligator with humps on his tail that is calling. They're always wanting me to go with them."

The rabbit looked out of the window and he heard some one laughing.

"That doesn't sound like a bad fox, nor yet an unpleasant alligator," said Mr. Longears. "Who is it wants me to come with them?"

"It is I—Susie Littletail, the rabbit girl," was the answer.

"And where do you want me to come?" asked Uncle Wiggily.

"To the woods, to pick some flowers," answered Susie. "The lady mouse teacher wants me to see how many kinds I can find. You know so much about the woods, Uncle Wiggily, that I wish you'd come with me."

"I will," said the nice rabbit gentleman. "Wait until I get my tall silk hat and my red, white and blue striped barber pole rheumatism crutch."

And, when he had them, off he started, holding Susie's paw in his, and limping along under the green trees and over the carpet of green moss.

Uncle Wiggily and the little rabbit girl found many kinds of flowers in the woods. There were violets, some white, some yellow and some purple, with others blue, like the ones Uncle Wiggily used to make blueing water for Nurse Jane's clothes. And there were red flowers and yellow ones, and some Jacks-in-their-pulpits, which are very queer flowers indeed.

"Here, Susie, is a new kind of blossom. Maybe you would like some of these," said Uncle Wiggily, pointing to a bush that was covered with little round, white balls.

"Oh, I didn't know the snow had lasted this long!" Susie cried. "I thought it had melted long ago."

"I don't see any snow," said Uncle Wiggily, looking around.

"On that bush," said Susie, pointing to the white one.

"Oh!" laughed the bunny uncle. "That does look like snow, to be sure. But it isn't, though the name of the flowers is snowdrop."

"Flowers! I don't call them flowers!" said Susie. "They are only white balls."

"Don't you want to pick any?" asked the rabbit.

"Thank you, no," Susie said. "I like prettier colored flowers than those, which are just plain white."

"Well, I like them, and I'll take some to Nurse Jane," spoke the bunny uncle. So he picked a bunch of the snowdrops and carried them in his paws, while Susie gathered the brighter flowers.

"I think those will be all teacher will want," said the little rabbit girl at last.

"Yes, we had better be getting home," spoke Uncle Wiggily. "Nurse Jane will soon have supper ready. Won't you come and eat with me, Susie?"

"Thank you, I will, Uncle Wiggily," and the little bunny girl clapped her paws; that is, as well as she could, on account of holding her flowers, for she loved to eat at Uncle Wiggily's hollow stump bungalow, as did all the animal children.

Well, Uncle Wiggily and Susie were going along and along through the woods, when, all of a sudden, as they passed a high rock, out from behind it jumped the bad old tail-pulling monkey.

"Ah, ha!" chattered the monkey chap. "I am just in time, I see."

"Time for what?" asked Uncle Wiggily, suspicious like.

"To pull your tails," answered the monkey. "I haven't had any tails to pull in a long while, and I must pull some. So, though you rabbits haven't very good tails, for pulling, I must do the best I can. Now come to me and have your tails pulled. Come on!"

"Oh, dear!" cried Susie. "I don't want my tail pulled, even if it is very short."

"Nor I mine," Uncle Wiggily said.

"That makes no manner of difference to me," chattered the monkey. "I'm a tail-pulling chap, and tails I must pull. So you might as well have it over with, now as later." And he spoke just like a dentist who wants to take your lolly-pop away from you.

"Pull our tails! Well, I guess you won't!" cried Uncle Wiggily suddenly. "Come on, Susie! Let's run away!"

As they passed a high rock, out from behind it
jumped the bad old tail-pulling monkey.

Before the monkey could grab them Uncle Wiggily and Susie started to run. But soon the monkey was running after them, crying:

"Stop! Stop! I must pull your tails!"

"But we don't want you to," answered Susie.

"Oh, but you must let me!" cried the monkey. Then he gave a great big, long, strong and double-jointed jump, like a circus clown going over the backs of fourteen elephants, and part of another one, and the monkey grabbed Uncle Wiggily by his ears.

"Oh, let go of me, if you please!" begged the bunny. "I thought you said you pulled tails and not ears."

"I do pull tails when I can get hold of them," said the malicious monkey. "But as I can't easily get hold of your tail, and as your ears are so large that I can easily grab them, I'll pull them instead. All ready now, a long pull, a strong pull and a pull altogether!"

"Stop!" cried the bunny uncle, just as the monkey was going to give the three kinds of pull at once. "Stop!"

"No!" answered the monkey. "No! No!"

"Yes! Yes!" cried the bunny uncle. "If you don't stop pulling my ears you'll freeze!" and with that the bunny uncle pulled out from behind him, where he had kept them hidden, the bunch of white snowdrops.

"Ah, ha!" cried Mr. Longears to the monkey. "You come from a warm country, where there is no snow or snowdrops. Now when you see these snow drops, shiver and shake—see how cold it is! Shiver and shake! Shake and shiver! Burr-r-r-r-r!"

Uncle Wiggily made believe the flowers were real snow, sort of shivering himself (pretend like) and the tail-pulling chap, who was very much afraid of cold and snow and ice, chattered and said:

"Oh, dear! Oh, how cold I am! Oh, I'm freezing. I am going back to my warm nest in the tree and not pull any tails until next summer!"

And then the monkey ran away, thinking the snowdrops Uncle Wiggily had picked were bits of real snow.

"I'm sorry I said the snowdrops weren't nice," spoke Susie, as she and Uncle Wiggily went safely home. "They are very nice. Only for them the monkey would have pulled our tails."

But he didn't, you see, and if the hookworm doesn't go to the moving pictures with the gold fish and forget to come back to play tag with the toy piano, I'll tell you next about Uncle Wiggily and the horse chestnut tree.

STORY XIII

UNCLE WIGGILY AND THE HORSE CHESTNUT

"Bang! Bango! Bunko! Bunk! Slam!"

Something made a big noise on the front porch of the hollow stump bungalow, where, in the woods, lived Uncle Wiggily Longears, the rabbit gentleman.

"My goodness!" cried Nurse Jane Fuzzy Wuzzy, the muskrat lady housekeeper. "I hope nothing has happened!"

"Well, from what I heard I should say it is quite certain that SOMETHING has happened," spoke the bunny uncle, sort of twisting his ears very anxious like.

"I only hope the chimney hasn't turned a somersault, and that the roof is not trying to play tag with the back steps," went on Miss Fuzzy Wuzzy, a bit scared like.

"I'll go see what it is," offered Uncle Wiggily, and as he went to the front door there, on the piazza, he saw Billie Wagtail, the little goat boy.

"Oh, good morning, Uncle Wiggily," spoke Billie, politely. "Here's a note for you. I just brought it."

"And did you bring all that noise with you?" Mr. Longears wanted to know.

"Well, yes, I guess I did," Billie said, sort of bashful like and shy as he wiggled his horns. "I was seeing how fast I could run, and I ran down hill and got going so lickity-split like that I couldn't stop. I fell right up your front steps, rattle-te-bang!"

"I should say it was rattle-te-bang!" laughed Uncle Wiggily. "But please don't do it again, Billie."

"I won't," promised the goat boy. "Grandpa Goosey Gander gave me that note to leave for you on my way to the store for my mother. And now I must hurry on," and Billie jumped off the porch and skipped along through the Woodland trees as happy as a huckleberry pie and a piece of cheese.

"What was it all about?" asked Nurse Jane, when Uncle Wiggily came in.

"Oh, just Billie Wagtail," answered the bunny uncle. "He brought a note from Grandpa Goosey, who wants me to come over and see him. I'll go. He has the epizootic, and can't get out, so he wants some one to talk to and to play checkers with him."

Off through the woods went Uncle Wiggily and he was almost at Grandpa Goosey's house when he heard some voices talking. One voice said:

"Oh, dear! How thirsty I am!"

"And so am I!" said another.

"Well, children, I am sorry," spoke a third voice, "but I cannot give you any water. I am thirsty myself, but we cannot drink until it rains, and it has not rained in a long, long time."

"Oh, dear! Oh, dear! Oh, dear!" cried the other voices again. "How thirsty we are!"

"That's too bad," thought Uncle Wiggily. "I would not wish even the bad fox to be thirsty. I must see if I can not be of some help."

So he peeked through the bushes and saw some trees.

"Was it you who were talking about being thirsty?" asked the rabbit gentleman, curious like.

"Yes," answered the big voice. "I am a horse chestnut tree, and these are my children," and the large tree waved some branches, like fingers, at some small trees growing under her.

"And they, I suppose, are pony chestnut trees," said Uncle Wiggily.

"That's what we are!" cried the little trees, "and we are very thirsty."

"Indeed they are," said the mother tree. "You see we are not like you animals. We cannot walk to a spring or well to get a drink when we are thirsty. We have to stay, rooted in one place, and wait for the rain, or until some one waters us."

"Well, some one is going to water you right away!" cried Uncle Wiggily in his jolly voice. "I'll bring you some water from the duck pond, which is near by."

Then, borrowing a pail from Mrs. Wibblewobble, the duck lady, Uncle Wiggily poured water all around the dry earth, in which grew the horse chestnut tree and the little pony trees.

"Oh! How fine that is!" cried the thirsty trees. "It is almost as nice as rain. You are very good, Uncle Wiggily," said the mother tree, "and if ever we can do you a favor we will."

"Thank you," spoke Uncle Wiggily, making a low bow with his tall silk hat. Then he went on to Grandpa Goosey's where he visited with his epizootic friend and played checkers.

On his way home through the woods, Uncle Wiggily was unpleasantly surprised when, all of a sudden out from behind a stone jumped a bad bear. He wasn't at all a good, nice bear like Beckie or Neddie Stubtail.

"Bur-r-r-r!" growled the bear at Uncle Wiggily. "I guess I'll scratch you."

"Oh, please don't," begged the bunny uncle.

"Yes, I shall!" grumbled the bear. "And I'll hug you, too!"

"Oh, no! I'd rather you wouldn't!" said the bunny uncle. For well he knew that a bear doesn't hug for love. It's more of a hard, rib-cracking squeeze than a hug. If ever a bear wants to hug you, just don't you let him. Of course if daddy or mother wants to hug, why, that's all right.

"Yes, I'm going to scratch you and hug you," went on the bad bear, "and after that—well, after that I guess I'll take you off to my den."

"Oh, please don't!" begged Uncle Wiggily, twinkling his nose and thinking that he might make the bear laugh. For if ever you can get a bear to laugh he won't hurt you a bit. Just remember that. Tickle him, or do anything to get him to laugh. But this bear wouldn't even smile. He just growled again and said:

"Well, here I come, Uncle Wiggily, to hug you!"

"Oh, no you don't!" all of a sudden cried a voice in the air.

"Ha! Who says I don't?" grumbled the bear, impolite like.

"I do," went on the voice. And the bear saw some trees waving their branches at him.

"Pooh! I'm not afraid of you!" growled the bear, and he made a rush for the bunny. "I'm not afraid of trees."

"Not afraid of us, eh? Well, you'd better be!" said the mother tree. "I'm a strong horse chestnut and these are my strong little ponies. Come on, children, we won't let the bear get Uncle Wiggily." Then the strong horse chestnut tree and the pony trees reached down with their powerful branches and, catching hold of the bear, they tossed him up in the air, far away over in the woods, at the same time pelting him with green, prickly horse chestnuts, and the bear came down ker-bunko in a bramble brier bush.

"Oh, wow!" cried the bear, as he felt his soft and tender nose being scratched. "I'll be good! I'll be good!"

And he was, for a little while, anyhow. So this shows you how a horse chestnut tree saved the bunny gentleman, and if the postman doesn't stick a stamp on our cat's nose so it can't eat molasses cake when it goes to the puppy dog's party, I'll tell you next about Uncle Wiggily and the pine tree.

STORY XIV

UNCLE WIGGILY AND THE PINE TREE

Uncle Wiggily Longears, the nice old gentleman rabbit, put on his tall silk hat, polished his glasses with the tip of his tail, to make them shiny so he could see better through them, and then, taking his red, white and blue striped rheumatism crutch down off the mantel, he started out of his hollow stump bungalow one day.

"Better take an umbrella, hadn't you?" asked Nurse Jane Fuzzy Wuzzy, the muskrat lady housekeeper. "It looks as though we might have an April shower."

"An umbrella? Yes, I think I will take one," spoke the bunny uncle, as he saw some dark clouds in the sky. "They look as though they might have rain in them."

"Are you going anywhere in particular?" asked the muskrat lady, as she tied her tail in a soft knot.

"No, not special," Uncle Wiggily answered. "May I have the pleasure of doing something for you?" he asked with a polite bow, like a little girl speaking a piece in school on Friday afternoon.

"Well," said Nurse Jane, "I have baked some apple dumplings with oranges inside, and I thought perhaps you might like to take one to Grandfather Goosey Gander to cheer him up."

"The very thing!" cried Uncle Wiggily, jolly-like. "I'll do it, Nurse Jane."

So with an apple dumpling carefully wrapped up in a napkin and put in a basket, Uncle Wiggily started off through the woods and over the fields to Grandpa Goosey's house.

"I wonder if I shall have an adventure today?" thought the rabbit gentleman as he waved his ears to and fro like the pendulum of a clock. "I think I would like one to give me an appetite for supper. I must watch for something to happen."

He looked all around the woods, but all he could see were some trees.

"I can't have any adventures with them," said the bunny uncle, "though the horse chestnut tree did help me the other day by tossing the bad bear over into the briar bush. But these trees are not like that."

Still Uncle Wiggily was to have an adventure with one of the trees very soon. Just you wait, now, and you shall hear about it.

Uncle Wiggily walked on a little farther and he heard a funny tapping noise in the woods.

"Tap! Tap! Tap! Tappity-tap-tap!" it sounded.

"My! Some one is knocking on a door trying to get in," thought the bunny. "I wonder who it can be?"

Just then he saw a big bird perched on the side of a pine tree, tapping with his bill.

"Tap! Tap! Tap!" went the bird.

"Excuse me," said the bunny uncle, "but you are making a mistake. No one lives in that tree."

"Oh, thank you, Uncle Wiggily. I know that no one lives here," said the bird. "But you see I am a woodpecker, and I am pecking holes in the tree to get some of the sweet juice, or sap. The sap is running in the trees now, for it is Spring. Later on I will tap holes in the bark to get at bugs and worms, when there is no more sap for me to eat."

And the woodpecker went on tapping, tapping, tapping.

"My! That is a funny way to get something to eat," said the bunny gentleman to himself. He watched the bird until it flew away, and then Uncle Wiggily was about to hop on to Grandpa Goosey's house when, all of a sudden, before he could run away, out popped the bad old bear once more.

"Ah, ha! We meet again, I see," growled the bear. "I was not looking for you, Mr. Longears, but all the same I am glad to meet you, for I want to eat you."

"Well," said Uncle Wiggily, sort of scratching his pink, twinkling nose with his ear, surprised like. "I can't exactly say I'm glad to see you, good Mr. Bear."

"No, I s'pose not," agreed the fuzzy creature. "But you are mistaken. I am the Bad Mr. Bear, not the Good."

"Oh, excuse me," said Uncle Wiggily. All the while he knew the bear was bad, but he hoped by calling him good, to make him so.

"I'm very bad!" growled the bear, "and I'm going to take you off to my den with me. Come along!"

"Oh, I don't want to," said the bunny uncle, shivering his tail.

"But you must!" growled the bear. "Come on, now!"

"Oh, dear!" cried Uncle Wiggily. "Will you let me go if I give you what's in my basket?" he asked, and he held up the basket with the nice orange apple turnover in it. "Let me go if I give you this," begged the bunny uncle.

"Maybe I will, and maybe I won't," said the bear, cunning like. "Let me see what it is."

He took the basket from Uncle Wiggily, and looking in, said:

"Ah, ha! An apple turnover-dumpling with oranges in it! I just love them! Ah, ha!"

"Oh," thought Uncle Wiggily. "I hope he eats it, for then maybe I can get away when he doesn't notice me. I hope he eats it!"

And the bear, leaning his back against the pine tree in which the woodpecker had been boring holes, began to take bites out of the apple dumpling which Nurse Jane had baked for Grandpa Goosey.

"Now's my chance to get away!" thought the bunny gentleman. But when he tried to hop softly off, as the bear was eating the sweet stuff, the bad creature saw him and cried:

"Ah, ha! No you don't! Come hack here!" and with his claws he pulled Uncle Wiggily close to him again.

Then the bunny uncle noticed that some sweet, sticky juice or gum, like that on fly paper, was running down the trunk of the tree from the holes the woodpecker had drilled in it.

"Oh, if the bear only leans back hard enough and long enough against that sticky pine tree," thought Mr. Longears, "he'll be stuck fast by his furry hair and he can't get me. I hope he sticks!"

And that is just what happened. The bear enjoyed eating the apple dumpling so much that he leaned back harder and harder against the sticky tree. His fur stuck fast in the gum that ran out. Finally the bear ate the last crumb of the dumpling.

"And now I'll get you!" he cried to the bunny uncle; "I'll get you!"

But did the bear get Uncle Wiggily? He did not. The bear tried to jump toward the rabbit, but could not. He was stuck fast to the sticky pine tree and Uncle Wiggily could now run safely back to his hollow stump bungalow to get another dumpling for Grandpa Goosey.

So the bear had no rabbit, after all, and all he did was to stay stuck fast to the pine tree until a big fox came along and helped him to get loose, and the bear cried "Wouch!" because his fur was pulled.

So Uncle Wiggily was all right, you see, after all, and very thankful he was to the pine tree for holding fast to the bear.

And in the next story, if our cat doesn't go hunting for the poll parrot's cracker in the gold fish bowl and get his whiskers all wet, I'll tell you about Uncle Wiggily and the green rushes.

STORY XV

UNCLE WIGGILY AND THE GREEN RUSHES

Once upon a time Uncle Wiggily Longears, the nice rabbit gentleman, was taking a walk in the woods, looking for an adventure, as he often did, when, as he happened to go past the hollow tree, where Billie and Johnnie Bushytail, the two squirrel boys lived, he saw them just poking their noses out of the front door, which was a knot-hole.

"Hello, boys!" called Uncle Wiggily. "Why haven't you gone to school today? It is time, I'm sure."

"Oh, we don't have to go today," answered Billie, as he looked at his tail to see if any chestnut burrs were sticking in it. But none was, I am glad to say.

"Don't have to go to school? Why not?" Uncle Wiggily wanted to know. "This isn't Saturday, is it?"

"No," spoke Johnnie. "But you see, Sister Sallie, our little squirrel sister, has the measles, and we can't go to school until she gets over them."

"And we don't know what to do to have some fun," went on Billie, "for lots of the animal children are home from school with the measles, and they can't be out to play with us. We've had the measles, so we can't get them the second time, but the animal boys and girls, who haven't broken out, don't want us to come and see them for fear we'll bring the red spots to them."

"I see," said Uncle Wiggily, laughing until his pink nose twinkled like a jelly roll. "So you can't have any fun? Well, suppose you come with me for a walk in the woods."

"Fine!" cried Billie and Johnnie and soon they were walking in the woods with the rabbit gentleman. They had not gone very far before, all of a sudden, they came to a place where a mud turtle gentleman had fallen on his back, and he could not turn over, right-side up again. He tried and tried, but he could not right himself.

"Oh, that is too bad!" cried Uncle Wiggily, when he saw what had happened. "I must help him to get right-side up again," which he did.

"Oh, thank you for putting me on my legs once more, Uncle Wiggily," said the mud turtle. "I would like to do you a favor for helping me, but all I have to give you are these," and in one claw he picked some green stalks growing near him, and handed them to the bunny uncle, afterward crawling away.

"Pooh! Those are no good!" cried Billie, the boy squirrel.

"I should say not!" laughed Johnnie, "They are only green rushes that grow all about in the woods, and we could give Uncle Wiggily all he wanted."

"Hush, boys! Don't talk that way," said the bunny uncle. "The mud turtle tried to do the best he could for me, and I am sure the green rushes are very nice. I'll take them with me. I may find use for them."

Billie and Johnnie wanted to laugh, for they thought green rushes were of no use at all. But Uncle Wiggily said to the squirrel boys:

"Billie and Johnnie, though green rushes, which grow in the woods and swamps are very common, still they are a wonderful plant. See how smooth they are when you rub them up and down. But if you rub them sideways they are as rough as a stiff brush or a nutmeg grater."

Well, Billie and Johnnie thought more of the rushes after that, but, as they walked on with Uncle Wiggily, when he had put them in his pocket, they could think of no way in which he could use them.

In a little while they came to where Mother Goose lived, and the dear old lady herself was out in front of her house, looking up and down the woodland path, anxious like.

"What is the matter?" asked Uncle Wiggily. "Are you looking for some of your lost ones—Little Bopeep or Tommy Tucker, who sings for his supper?"

"Well, no, not exactly," answered Mother Goose. "I sent Simple Simon to the store to get me a scrubbing brush, so I could clean the kitchen floor. But he hasn't come back, and I am afraid he has gone fishing in his mother's pail, to try to catch a whale. Oh, dear! My kitchen is so dirty that it needs scrubbing right away. But I cannot do it without a scrubbing brush."

"Ha! Say no more!" cried Uncle Wiggily in his jolly voice. "I have no scrubbing brush, but I have a lot of green rushes the mud turtle gave me for turning him right-side up. The rushes are as rough as a scrubbing brush, and will do just as nicely to clean your kitchen."

"Oh, thank you! I'm sure they will," said Mother Goose. So she took the green rushes from Uncle Wiggily and by using them with soap and water soon her kitchen floor was scrubbed as clean as an eggshell, for the green, rough stems scraped off all the dirt.

Then Mother Goose thanked Uncle Wiggily very much, and Billie and Johnnie sort of looked at one another with blinking eyes, for they saw that green rushes are of some use in this world after all.

And if the strawberry jam doesn't go to the moving pictures with the bread and butter and forget to come home for supper, I'll tell you next about Uncle Wiggily and the bee tree.

STORY XVI

UNCLE WIGGILY AND THE BEE TREE

"Well, you're off again, I see!" spoke Nurse Jane Fuzzy Wuzzy, the muskrat lady housekeeper, one morning, as she saw Uncle Wiggily Longears, the rabbit gentleman, starting away from his hollow stump bungalow. He was limping on his red, white and blue striped barber pole rheumatism crutch, that Miss Fuzzy Wuzzy had gnawed for him out of a cornstalk. "Off again!" she cried.

"Yes, off again," said Uncle Wiggily. "I must have my adventure, you know."

"I hope it will be a pleasant one today," went on Nurse Jane.

"So do I," said Uncle Wiggily, and away he went hopping over the fields and through the woods. He had not gone very far before he heard a queer buzzing sound, and a sort of splashing in the water and a tiny voice cried:

"Help! Help! Save me! I am drowning!"

"My goodness me sakes alive and some horse radish lollypops!" cried the bunny uncle. "Some one drowning? I don't see any water around here, though I do hear some splashing. Who are you?" he cried. "And where are you, so that I may save you?"

"Here I am, right down by your foot!" was the answer. "I am a honey bee, and I have fallen into this Jack-in-the pulpit flower, which is full of water. Please get me out!"

"To be sure I will!" cried Mr. Longears, and then, stooping down he carefully lifted the poor bee out of the water in the Jack-in-the-pulpit.

The Jack is a plant that looks like a little pitcher and it holds water. In the middle is a green stem, that is called Jack, because he looks like a minister preaching in the pulpit. The Jack happened to be out when the bee fell in the water that had rained in the plant-pitcher, or Jack himself would have saved the honey chap. But Uncle Wiggily did it just as well.

"Oh, thank you so much for not letting me drown," said the bee, as she dried her wings in the sun on a big green leaf. "I was on my way to the hive tree with a load of honey when I stopped for a drink. But I leaned over too far and fell in. I can not thank you enough!"

"Oh, once is enough!" cried Uncle Wiggily in his most jolly voice. "But did I understand you to say you lived in a hive-tree?"

"Yes, a lot of us bees have our hive in a hollow tree in the woods, not far away. It is there we store the honey we gather from Summer flowers, so we will have something to eat in the Winter when there are no blossoms. Would you like to see the bee tree?"

"Indeed, I would," Uncle Wiggily said.

"Follow me, then," buzzed the bee. "I will fly on ahead, very slowly, and you can follow me through the woods."

Uncle Wiggily did so, and soon he heard a great buzzing sound, and he saw hundreds of bees flying in and out of a hollow tree. At first some of the bees were going to sting the bunny uncle, but his little friend cried:

"Hold on, sisters! Don't sting this rabbit gentleman. He is Uncle Wiggily and he saved me from being drowned."

So the bees did not sting the bunny uncle, but, instead, gave him a lot of honey, in a little box made of birch bark, which he took home to Nurse Jane.

"Oh, I had the sweetest adventure!" he said to her, and he told her about the bee tree and the honey, which he and the muskrat lady ate on their carrot cake for dinner.

It was about a week after this, and Uncle Wiggily was once more in the woods, looking for an adventure, when, all at once a big bear jumped out from behind a tree and grabbed him.

"Oh, dear!" cried Uncle Wiggily. "Why did you do that? Why have you caught me, Mr. Bear?"

"Because I am going to carry you off to my den," answered the bear. "I am hungry, and I have been looking for something to eat. You came along just in time. Come on!"

The hear was leading Uncle Wiggily away when the bunny uncle happened to think of something, and it was this—that bears are very fond of sweet things.

"Would you not rather eat some honey than me?" Uncle Wiggily asked of the bear.

"Much rather," answered the shaggy creature, "but where is the honey?" he asked, cautious like and foxy.

"Come with me and I will show you where it is," went on the bunny uncle, for he felt sure that his friends the bees, would give the bear honey so the bad animal would let the rabbit gentleman go.

Uncle Wiggily led the way through the wood to the bee tree, the bear keeping hold of him all the while. Pretty soon a loud buzzing was heard, and when they came to where the honey was stored in the hollow tree, all of a sudden out flew hundreds of bees, and they stung the bear so hard all over, especially on his soft and tender nose, that the bear cried:

"Wow! Wouch! Oh, dear!" and, letting go of the rabbit, ran away to jump in the ice water to cool off.

But the bees did not sting Uncle Wiggily, for they liked him, and he thanked them for driving away the bear. So everything came out all right, you see, and if the foot-stool gets up to the head of the class and writes its name on the blackboard, with pink chalk, I'll tell you next about Uncle Wiggily and the dogwood tree.

STORY XVII

UNCLE WIGGILY AND THE DOGWOOD

"Where are you going, Uncle Wiggily?" asked Nurse Jane Fuzzy Wuzzy, the muskrat lady housekeeper, as the nice old rabbit gentleman started out from his hollow stump bungalow one afternoon.

"Oh, just for a walk in the woods," he answered. "Neddie Stubtail, the little bear boy, told me last night that there were many adventures in the forest, and I want to see if I can find one."

"My goodness! You seem very fond of adventures!" said Miss Fuzzy Wuzzy.

"I am," went on Uncle Wiggily, with a smile that made his pink nose twinkle and his whiskers sort of chase themselves around the back of his neck, as though they were playing tag with his collar button. "I just love to have adventures."

"Well, while you are out walking among the trees would you mind doing me a favor?" asked Nurse Jane.

"I wouldn't mind in the least," spoke the bunny uncle. "What would you like me to do?"

"Just leave this thimble at Mrs. Bow Wow's house. I borrowed the dog lady's thimble to use when I couldn't find mine, but now that I have my own back again I'll return hers."

"Where was yours?" Uncle Wiggily wanted to know.

"Jimmie Caw-Caw, the crow boy, had picked it up to hide under the pump," answered Nurse Jane. "Crows, you know, like to pick up bright and shining things."

"Yes, I remember," said Uncle Wiggily. "Very well, I'll give Mrs. Bow Wow her thimble," and off the old gentleman rabbit started, limping along on his red, white and blue striped rheumatism crutch, that Nurse Jane Fuzzy Wuzzy had gnawed for him out of a bean-pole. Excuse me, I mean corn stalk.

When Uncle Wiggily came to the place where Jackie and Peetie Bow Wow, the little puppy dog boys lived, he saw Mrs. Bow Wow, the dog lady, out in front of the kennel house looking up and down the path that led through the woods.

"Were you looking for me?" asked Uncle Wiggily, making a low and polite bow with his tall silk hat.

"Looking for you? Why, no, not specially," said Mrs. Bow Wow, "though I am always glad to see you."

"I thought perhaps you might be looking for your thimble," went on the bunny uncle. "Nurse Jane has sent it back to you."

"Oh, thank you!" said the mother of the puppy dog boys. "I'm glad to get my thimble back, but I was really looking for Peetie and Jackie."

"You don't mean to say they have run away, do you?" asked Uncle Wiggily, in surprise.

"No, not exactly run away. But they have not come home from school, though the lady mouse, who teaches in the hollow stump, must have let the animal children out long ago."

"She did," Uncle Wiggily said. "I came past the hollow stump school on my way here, and every one was gone."

"Then where can Jackie and Peetie be keeping themselves?" asked Mrs. Bow Wow. "Oh, I'm so worried about them!"

"Don't be worried or frightened," said Uncle Wiggily, kindly. "I'll go look for them for you."

"Oh, if you will I'll be so glad!" cried Mrs. Bow Wow. "And if you find them please tell them to come home at once."

"I will," promised the bunny uncle.

Giving the dog lady her thimble, Uncle Wiggily set off through the woods to look for Jackie and Peetie Bow Wow. On every side of the woodland path he peered, under trees and bushes and around the corners of moss-covered rocks and big stumps.

But no little puppy dog chaps could he find.

All at once, as Mr. Longears was going past an old log he heard a rustling in the bushes, and a voice said:

"Well, we nearly caught them, didn't we?"

"We surely did," said another voice. "And I think if we race after them once more we'll certainly have them. Let's rest here a bit, and then chase those puppy dogs some more. That Jackie is a good runner."

"I think Peetie is better," said the other voice. "Anyhow, they both got away from us."

"Ha! This must be Peetie and Jackie Bow Wow they are talking about," said Uncle Wiggily to himself. "This sounds like trouble. So the puppy dogs were chased, were they? I must see by whom."

He peeked through the bushes, and there he saw two big, bad foxes, whose tongues were hanging out over their white teeth, for the foxes had run far and they were tired.

"I see how it is," Uncle Wiggily thought. "The foxes chased the little puppy dogs as they were coming from school and Jackie and Peetie have run somewhere and hidden. I must find them."

Just then one of the foxes cried:

"Come on. Now we'll chase after those puppies, and get them. Come on!"

"Ha! I must go, too!" thought Uncle Wiggily. "Maybe I can scare away the foxes, and save Jackie and Peetie."

So the foxes ran and Uncle Wiggily also ran, and pretty soon the rabbit gentleman came to a place in the woods where grew a tree with big white blossoms on it, and in the center the blossoms were colored a dark red.

"Ha! There are the puppy boys under that tree!" cried one fox, and, surely enough, there, right under the tree, Jackie and Peetie were crouched, trembling and much frightened.

"We'll get them!" cried the other fox. "Come on!"

And then, all of a sudden, as the foxes leaped toward the poor little puppy dog boys, that tree began to hark and growl and it cried out loud:

"Get away from here, you bad foxes! Leave Jackie and Peetie alone! Wow! Bow-wow! Gurr-r-r-r!" and the tree barked and roared so like a lion that the foxes were frightened and were glad enough to run away, taking their tails with them. Then Jackie and Peetie came safely out, and thanked the tree for taking care of them.

The tree barked and roared so like a lion that the foxes
were frightened and were glad enough to run away.

"Oh, you are welcome," said the tree. "I am the dogwood tree, you know, so why should I not bark and growl to scare foxes, and take care of you little puppy chaps? Come to me again whenever any bad foxes chase you." And Peetie and Jackie said they would.

So Uncle Wiggily, after also thanking the tree, took the doggie boys home, and they told him how the foxes had chased them soon after they came from school, so they had to run.

But everything came out all right, you see, and if the black cat doesn't dip his tail in the ink, and make chalk marks all over the piano, I'll tell you next about Uncle Wiggily and the hazel nuts.

STORY XVIII

UNCLE WIGGILY AND THE HAZEL NUTS

"Going out again, Uncle Wiggily?" asked Nurse Jane Fuzzy Wuzzy, one morning, as she saw the rabbit gentleman taking his red, white and blue-striped rheumatism crutch down off the clock shelf.

"Well, yes, Janie, I did think of going out for a little stroll in the forest," answered the bunny uncle, talking like a phonograph. What he meant was that he was going for a walk in the woods, but he thought he'd be polite about it, and stylish, just for once.

"Don't forget your umbrella," went on Nurse Jane. "It looks to me very much as though there would be a storm."

"I think you're right," Uncle Wiggily said. "Our April showers are not yet over. I shall take my umbrella."

So, with his umbrella, and the rheumatism crutch which Nurse Jane had gnawed for him out of a cornstalk, off started the bunny uncle, hopping along over the fields and through the woods.

Pretty soon Uncle Wiggily met Johnnie Bushytail, the squirrel boy.

"Where are you going, Johnnie?" asked the rabbit gentleman. "Are you here in the woods, looking for an adventure? That's what I'm doing."

"No, Uncle Wiggily," answered the squirrel boy. "I'm not looking for an adventure. I'm looking for hazel nuts."

"Hazel nuts?" cried the bunny uncle in surprise.

"Yes," went on Johnnie. "You know they're something like chestnuts, only without the prickly burrs, and they're very good to eat. They grow on bushes, instead of trees. I'm looking for some to eat. They are nice, brown, shiny nuts."

"Good!" cried the rabbit gentleman. "We'll go together looking for hazel nuts, and perhaps we may also find an adventure. I'll take the adventure and you can take the hazel nuts."

"All right!" laughed Johnnie, and off they started.

On and over the fields and through the woods went the bunny uncle and Johnnie, until, just as they were close to the place where some extra early new kind of Spring hazel nuts grew on bushes, there was a noise behind a big black stump—and suddenly out pounced a bear!

"Oh, hello, Neddie Stubtail!" called Johnnie. And he was just going up and shake paws when Uncle Wiggily cried:

"Look out, Johnnie! Wait a minute! That isn't your friend Neddie!"

"Isn't it?" asked Johnnie, surprised-like, and he drew back.

"No, it's a bad old bear—not our nice Neddie, at all! And I think he is going to chase us! Get ready to run!"

So Johnnie Bushytail and Uncle Wiggily got ready to run. And it was a good thing they did, for just then the bear gave a growl, like a lollypop when it falls off the stick, and the bear said:

"Ah, ha! And oh, ho! A rabbit and a squirrel! Fine for me! Tag—your it!" he cried, and he made a jump for Uncle Wiggily and Johnnie.

But do you s'pose the bunny uncle and the squirrel boy stayed there to be caught? Indeed, they did not!

"Over this way! Quick!" cried Johnnie. "Here is a hazel nut bush, Uncle Wiggily. We can hide under that and the bear can't get us!"

"Good!" said the bunny uncle. And he and Johnnie quickly ran and hid under the hazel nut bush, which was nearby.

The bear looked all around as he heard Uncle Wiggily and Johnnie running away, and when he saw where they had gone he laughed until his whiskers twinkled, almost like the rabbit gentleman's pink nose, and then the bear said:

"Ha, ha! and Ho, ho! So you thought you could get away from me that way, did you? Well, you can't. I can see you hiding under that bush almost as plainly as I can see the sun shining. Here I come after you."

"Oh, dear!" cried Uncle Wiggily. "What shall we do, Johnnie? I don't want the bear to get you or me."

"And I don't either," spoke the little squirrel boy.

"I wonder if I could scare him away with my umbrella, Johnnie?" went on Uncle Wiggily. "I might if I could make believe it was a gun. Have you any talcum powder to shoot?"

"No," said Johnnie, sadly, "I have not, I am sorry to say."

"Have you any bullets?" asked the bunny uncle.

"No bullets, either," answered Johnnie, more sadly.

"Then I don't see anything for us to do but let the bear get us," sorrowfully said Mr. Longears. "Here he comes, Johnnie."

"But he sha'n't get us!" quickly cried the squirrel boy, as the bear made a jump for the bush under which the bunny and Johnnie were hiding. "He sha'n't get us!"

"Why not?" asked Uncle Wiggily.

"Because," said Johnnie, "I have just thought of something. You asked me for bullets a while ago. I have none, but the hazel nut bush has. Come, good Mr. Hazel Bush, will you save us from the bear?" asked Johnnie.

"Right gladly will I do that," the kind bush said.

"Then, when he comes for us!" cried Johnnie, "just rattle down, all over on him, all the hard nuts you can let fall. They will hit him on his ears, and on his soft and tender nose, and that will make him run away and leave us alone."

"Good!" whispered the hazel nut bush, rustling its leaves. "But what about you and Uncle Wiggily? If I rattle the nuts on the bear they will also fall on you two, as long as you are hiding under me."

"Have no fear of that!" said the bunny uncle. "I have my umbrella, and I will raise that and keep off the falling nuts."

Then the bear, with a growl, made a dash to get Uncle Wiggily and Johnnie. But the hazel bush shivered and shook himself and "Rattle-te-bang! Bung-bung! Bang!" down came the hazel nuts all over the bear.

"Oh, wow!" he cried, as they hit him on his soft and tender nose. "Oh, wow! I guess I'd better run away. It's hailing!"

And he did run. And because of Uncle Wiggily's umbrella held over his head, the nuts did not hurt him or Johnnie at all. And when the bear had run far away the squirrel boy gathered all the nuts he wanted, and he and Uncle Wiggily went safely home. And the bear's nose was sore for a week.

So if the hickory nut cake doesn't try to sit in the same seat with the apple pie and get all squeezed like a lemon pudding, I'll tell you next about Uncle Wiggily and Susie's dress.

STORY XIX

UNCLE WIGGILY AND SUSIE'S DRESS

Uncle Wiggily Longears, the nice old gentleman rabbit, was reading the paper in his hollow stump bungalow, in the woods, while Nurse Jane Fuzzy Wuzzy, the muskrat lady house-keeper, was out in the kitchen washing the dinner dishes one afternoon.

All of a sudden Uncle Wiggily fell asleep because he was reading a bed-time story in the paper, and while he slept he heard a noise at the front door, which sounded like:

"Rat-a-tat-tat! Rat-a-tat-tat!"

"My goodness!" suddenly exclaimed Uncle Wiggily, awakening out of his sleep. "That sounds like the forest woodpecker bird making holes in a tree."

"No, it isn't that," spoke Nurse Jane. "It's some one tapping at our front door. I can't answer because my paws are all covered with soapy-suds dishwater."

"Oh, I'll go," said Uncle Wiggily, and laying aside the paper over which he had fallen asleep, he opened the door. On the porch stood Susie Littletail, the rabbit girl.

"Why, hello Susie!" exclaimed the bunny uncle. "Where are you going with your nice new dress?" for Susie did have on a fine new waist and skirt, or maybe it was made in one piece for all I know. And her new dress had on it ruffles and thing-a-ma-bobs and curley-cues and insertions and Georgette crepe and all sorts of things like that.

"Where are you going, Susie?" asked Uncle Wiggily.

"I am going to a party," answered the little rabbit girl. "Lulu and Alice Wibblewobble, the duck girls, are going to have a party, and they asked me to come. So I came for you."

"But I'm not going to the party!" exclaimed Uncle Wiggily. "I haven't been invited."

"That doesn't make any difference," spoke Susie with a laugh. "You know they'll be glad to see you, anyhow. And I know Lulu meant to ask you, only she must have forgotten about it, because there is so much to do when you have a party."

"I know there is," Uncle Wiggily said, "and I don't blame Lulu and Alice a bit for not asking me. Anyhow I couldn't go, for I promised to come over this afternoon and play checkers with Grandfather Goosey Gander."

"Oh, but won't you walk with me to the party?" asked Susie, sort of teasing like. "I'm afraid to go through the woods alone, because Johnnie Bushytail, the squirrel boy, said you and he met a bear there yesterday."

"We did!" laughed Uncle Wiggily. "But the hazel bush drove him away by showering nuts on his nose."

"Well, I might not be so lucky as to have a hazelnut bush to help me," spoke Susie. "So I'd be very glad if you would walk through the woods with me. You can scare away the bear if we meet him."

"How?" asked Uncle Wiggily. "With my red, white and blue crutch or my umbrella?"

"With this popgun, which shoots toothpowder," said Susie. "It belongs to Sammie, my brother, but he let me take it. We'll bring the popgun with us, Uncle Wiggily, and scare the bear."

"All right," said the bunny uncle. "That's what we'll do. I'll go as far as the Wibblewobble duck house with you and leave you there at the party."

This made Susie very glad and happy, and soon she and Uncle Wiggily were going through the woods together. Susie's new dress was very fine and she kept looking at it as she hopped along.

All of a sudden, as the little rabbit girl and the bunny uncle were going along through the woods, they came to a mud puddle.

"Look out, now!" said Uncle Wiggily. "Don't fall in that, Susie."

"I won't," said the little rabbit girl. "I can easily jump across it."

But when she tried to, alas! Likewise unhappiness. Her hind paws slipped and into the mud puddle she fell with her new dress. "Splash!" she went.

"Oh, dear!" cried Susie.

"Oh, my!" exclaimed Uncle Wiggily.

"Look at my nice, new dress," went on Susie. "It isn't at all nice and new now. It's all mud and water and all splashed up, and—oh, dear! Isn't it too bad!"

"Yes, besides two it is even six, seven and eight bad," said Uncle Wiggily sadly. "Oh, dear!"

"I can't go to the Wibblewobble party this way," cried Susie. "I'll have to go back home to get another dress, and it won't be my new one—and oh, dear!"

"Perhaps I can wipe off the mud with some leaves and moss," Uncle Wiggily spoke. "I'll try."

But the more he rubbed at the mud spots on Susie's dress the worse they looked.

"Oh, you can't do it, Uncle Wiggily!" sighed the little rabbit girl.

"No, I don't believe I can," Uncle Wiggily admitted, sadly-like and sorry.

"Oh, dear!" cried Susie. "Whatever shall I do? I can't go to a party looking like this! I just must have a new dress."

Uncle Wiggily thought for a minute. Then, through the woods, he spied a tree with white, shiny bark on, just like satin.

"Ha! I know what to do!" he cried. "That is a white birch tree. Indians make boats of the bark, and from it I can also make a new dress for you, Susie. Or, at least, a sort of dress, or apron, to go over the dress you have on, and so cover the mud spots."

"Please do!" begged Susie.

"I will!" promised Uncle Wiggily, and he did.

He stripped off some bark from the birch tree and he sewed the pieces together with ribbon grass, and some needles from the pine tree. And when Susie put on the bark dress over her party one, not a mud spot showed!

"Oh, that's fine, Uncle Wiggily!" she cried. "Now I can go to the Wibblewobbles!"

And so she went, and the bad bear never came out to so much as growl, nor did the fox, so the popgun was not needed. And all the girls at the party thought Susie's dress that Uncle Wiggily had made was just fine.

So if the rain drop doesn't fall out of bed, and stub its toe on the rocking chair, which might make it so lame that it couldn't dance, I'll tell you next about Uncle Wiggily and Tommie's kite.

STORY XX

UNCLE WIGGILY AND TOMMIE'S KITE

"Uncle Wiggily, have you anything special to do today?" asked Tommie Kat, the little kitten boy, one morning as he knocked on the door of the hollow stump bungalow, where Mr. Longears, the rabbit gentleman, lived.

"Anything special to do? Why, no, I guess not," answered the bunny uncle. "I just have to go walking to look for an adventure to happen to me, and then—"

"Didn't you promise to go to the five and ten cent store for me, and buy me a pair of diamond earrings?" asked Nurse Jane Fuzzy Wuzzy, the muskrat lady housekeeper.

"Oh, so I did!" cried Uncle Wiggily. "I had forgotten about that. But I'll go. What was it you wanted of me?" he asked Tommie Kat, who was making a fishpole of his tail by standing it straight up in the air.

"Oh, I wanted you to come and help me build a kite, and then come with me and fly it," said the kitten boy. "Could you do that, Uncle Wiggily?"

"Well, perhaps I could," said the bunny uncle. "I will first go to the store and get Nurse Jane's diamond earrings. Then, on the way back, I'll stop and help you with your kite. And after that is done I'll go along and see if I can find an adventure."

"That will be fun!" cried Tommie. "I have everything all ready to make the kite—paper, sticks, paste and string. We'll make a big one and fly it away up in the air."

So off through the woods started Uncle Wiggily and Tommie to the five and ten cent store. There they bought the diamond earrings for

Nurse Jane, who wanted to wear them to a party Mrs. Cluck-Cluck, the hen lady, was going to have next week.

"And now to make the kite!" cried Tommie, as he and Uncle Wiggily reached the house where the Kat family lived.

The bunny uncle and the little kitten boy cut out some red paper in the shape of a kite. Then they pasted it on the crossed sticks, which were tied together with string.

"The kite is almost done," said Uncle Wiggily, as he held it up. "And can you tell me, Tommie, why your kite is like Buddy, the guinea pig boy?"

"Can I tell you why my kite is like Buddy, the guinea pig boy?" repeated Tommie, like a man in a minstrel show. "No, Uncle Wiggily, I can not. Why is my kite like Buddy, the guinea pig boy?"

"Because," laughed the old rabbit gentleman, "this kite has no tail and neither has Buddy."

"Ha, ha!" exclaimed Tommie. "That's right!"

For guinea pigs have no tails, you know, though if you ask me why I can't tell you. Some kites do have tails, though, and others do not.

Anyhow, Tommie's kite, without a tail, was soon finished, and then he and Uncle Wiggily went to a clear, open place in the fields, near the woods, to fly it.

There was a good wind blowing, and when Uncle Wiggily raised the kite up off the ground, Tommie ran, holding the string that was fast to the kite and up and up and up it went in the air. Soon it was sailing quite near the clouds, almost like Uncle Wiggily's airship, only, of course, no one rode on the kite.

"Have you any more string, Uncle Wiggily?" asked the kitten boy, after a bit.

"String, Tommie? What for?"

"Well, I want to make my kite string longer so it will go up higher. But if you have none I'll run home and get some myself. Will you hold the kite while I'm gone?"

"To be sure I will," said Uncle Wiggily. So he took hold of the string of Tommie's kite, which was now quite high in the air. And, sitting down on the ground, Uncle Wiggily held the kite from running away while Tommie went for more string.

It was a nice, warm, summer day, and so pleasant in the woods, with the little flies buzzing about, that, before he knew it Uncle Wiggily had fallen asleep. His pink nose stopped twinkling, his ears folded themselves down like a slice of bread and jam, and Uncle Wiggily's eyes closed.

All of a sudden he was awakened by feeling himself being pulled. At first he thought it was the skillery-scalery alligator, or the bad fox trying to drag him off to his den, and Uncle Wiggily, opening his eyes, cried:

"Here! Stop that if you please! Don't pull me so!"

But when he looked around he could see no one, and then he knew it was Tommie's kite, flying up in the air, that was doing the pulling.

The wind was blowing hard now, and as Uncle Wiggily had the kite string wound around his paws, of course he was pulled almost off his feet.

"Ha! That kite is a great puller!" said the bunny uncle. "I must look out or it might pull me up to the clouds. I had better fasten the string to this old stump. The kite can't pull that up."

So the rabbit gentleman fastened the kite cord to the stout old stump, winding it around two or three times, and he kept the loose end of the string in his paw.

Uncle Wiggily was just going to sleep again, and he was wondering why it took Tommie so long to find more string for the kite, when, all of a sudden, there was a rustling in the bushes, and out jumped the bad old babboon, who had, once before, made trouble for the bunny uncle.

"Ah, ha!" jabbered the babboon. "This time I have caught you. You can't get away from me now. I am going to take you off to my den."

"Oh, please don't!" begged Uncle Wiggily.

"Yes, I shall, too!" blabbered the babboon. "Off to my den you shall go—you shall go—you shall go. Off to my den. Oh, hold on!" cried the bad creature. "That isn't the song I wanted to sing. That's the London Bridge song. I want the one about the dinner bell is ringing in the bread box this fine day. And the dinner bell is ringing for to take you far away, Uncle Wiggily."

"Ah, then I had better go to my dinner," said the bunny uncle, sadly.

"No! You will go with me!" cried the babboon. "Come along now. I'm going to take you away."

"Well, if I must go, I suppose I must," Uncle Wiggily said, looking at the kite string, which was pulling at the stump very hard now. "But before you take me away would you mind pulling down Tommie's kite?" asked the bunny uncle. "I'll leave it for him."

"Yes, I'll pull the kite down," said the babboon.

"Maybe you will," thought Uncle Wiggily, laughing to himself. "And maybe you won't."

The bad babboon monkey chap unwound the string from the stump, but no sooner had he started to pull in the kite than there came a very strong puff of wind.

Up, up and up into the air blew the kite and,
as the string was tangled around the babboon's paws,
it took him up with it.

Up, up and up into the air blew the kite and, as the string was tangled around the babboon's paws, it took him up with it, and though he cried out: "Stop! Stop! Stop!" the kite could not stop, nor the babboon either.

"Well, I guess you won't bother me any more," said Uncle Wiggily, as he looked at the babboon, who was only a speck in the sky now; a very little speck, being carried away by the kite.

And the babboon did not come back to bother Uncle Wiggily, at least for a long time. Tommie felt badly when he found his kite blown away. But he was glad Uncle Wiggily had been saved, and he and the bunny uncle soon made a new kite, better than the first. They had lots of fun flying it.

And in the story after this, if the chocolate pudding doesn't hide in the coal bin, where the cook can't find it to put the whipped cream on, I'll tell you about Uncle Wiggily and Johnnie's marbles.

STORY XXI

UNCLE WIGGILY AND JOHNNIE'S MARBLES

It was a nice, warm spring day, when the ground in the woods where the animal boys and girls lived was soft, for all the frost had melted out of it; and, though it was a little too early to go barefoot, it was not too early to play marbles.

Johnnie and Billie Bushytail, the squirrels; Sammie Littletail, the rabbit, and Jimmie Wibblewobble, the duck, were having a game under the trees, not far from the hollow stump bungalow which was the house of Uncle Wiggily Longears, the bunny gentleman.

"First shot agates!" cried Johnnie.

"No, I'm going to shoot first!" chattered his brother Billie.

"Huh! I hollered it before either of you," quacked Jimmie, the duck boy, and he tossed some red, white and blue striped marbles on the ground in the ring. The marbles were just the color of Uncle Wiggily's rheumatism crutch.

The animal boys began playing, but they made so much noise, crying "Fen!" and "Ebbs!" and "Knuckle down!" that Nurse Jane Fuzzy Wuzzy, the muskrat lady housekeeper, went to the bungalow door and called:

"Boys! Boys! Will you please be a little quiet? Uncle Wiggily is lying down taking a nap, and I don't want you to wake him up with your marbles."

"Oh, I don't mind!" cried the bunny uncle, unfolding his ears from his vest pockets, where he always tucked them when he went to sleep, so the flies would not tickle him. "It's about time I got up," he said.

"So the boys are playing marbles, eh? Well, I'll go out and watch them. It will make me think of the days when I was a spry young bunny chap, hopping about, spinning my kites and flying my tops."

"I guess you are a little bit twisted; are you not?" asked Nurse Jane, politely.

"Oh, so I am," said Uncle Wiggily. "I mean flying my kite and spinning my top."

Then he pinkled his twink nose—Ah! you see that's the time I was twisted—I mean he twinkled his pink nose, Uncle Wiggily did, and out he went to watch the animal boys play marbles.

Billie, Johnnie and Jimmie, as well as Sammie, wanted the bunny uncle to play also, but he said his rheumatism hurt too much to bend over. So he just watched the marble game, until it was time for the boys to go home. And then Johnnie cried:

"Oh, I forgot! I have to go to the store for a loaf of bread for supper. Come on, fellows, with me, will you?"

But neither Jimmie, nor Sammie nor Billie wanted to go with Johnnie, so he started off through the woods to the store alone, when Uncle Wiggily cried:

"Wait a minute, Johnnie, and I'll go with you. I haven't had my walk this day, and I have had no adventure at all. I'll go along and see what happens."

"Oh, that will be nice!" chattered Johnnie, who did not like to go to the store alone. So, putting his marbles in the bag in which he carried them, he ran along beside Uncle Wiggily.

They had not gone far when, all of a sudden, there came a strong puff of wind, and, before Uncle Wiggily could hold his hat down over his ears, it was blown off his head. I mean his hat was—not his ears.

Away through the trees the tall silk hat was blown.

"Oh, dear!" cried the bunny uncle. "I guess I am not going to have a nice adventure today."

"I'll get your hat for you, Uncle Wiggily!" said Johnnie kindly. "You hold my bag of marbles so I can run faster, and I'll get the hat for you."

Tossing the rabbit gentleman the marbles, away scampered Johnnie after the hat. But the wind kept on blowing it, and the squirrel boy had to run a long way.

"Well, I hope he gets it and brings it back to me," thought Uncle Wiggily, as he sat down on a green, moss-covered stone to wait for the squirrel boy. And, while he was waiting the bunny uncle opened the bag and looked at Johnnie's marbles. There were green ones, and blue and red and pink—very pretty, all of them.

"I wonder if I have forgotten how to play the games I used to enjoy when I was a boy rabbit?" thought the bunny gentleman. "Just now, when no one is here in tile woods to laugh at me, I think I'll try and see how well I can shoot marbles."

So he marked out a ring on the ground, and putting some marbles in the center began shooting at them with another marble, just the way you boys do.

"Ha! A good shot!" cried the bunny uncle, as he knocked two marbles out of the ring at once. "I am not so old as I thought I was, even if I have the rheumatism."

He was just going to shoot again when a growling voice over behind a bush said:

"Well, you will not have it much longer."

"Have what much longer?" asked Uncle Wiggily, and glancing up, there he saw a big bear, not at all polite looking.

"You won't have the rheumatism much longer," the bear said.

"Why not?" Uncle Wiggily wanted to know.

"Because," answered the bear, "I am going to eat you up and the rheumatism, too. Here I come!" and he made a jump for the bunny uncle. But did he catch him?

That bear did not, for he stepped on one of the round marbles, which rolled under his paw and he fell down ker-punko! on his nose-o!

Uncle Wiggily started to run away, but he did not like to go and leave Johnnie's marbles on the ground, so he stayed to pick them up, and by then the bear stood up on his hind legs again, and grabbed the bunny uncle in his sharp claws.

"Ah ha! Now I have you!" said the bear, grillery and growlery like.

"Yes, I see you have," sadly spoke Uncle Wiggily. "But before you take me off to your den, which I suppose you will do, will you grant me one favor?"

"Yes, and only one," growled the bear. "Be quick about it! What is it?"

"Will you let me have one more shot?" asked the bunny uncle. "I want to see if I can knock the other marbles out of the ring."

"Well, I see no harm in that," slowly grumbled the bear. "Go ahead. Shoot!"

Uncle Wiggily picked out the biggest shooter in Johnnie's bag. Then he took careful aim, but, instead of aiming at the marbles in the ring he aimed at the soft and tender nose of the bear.

"Bing!" went the marble which Uncle Wiggily shot, right on the bear's nose. "Bing!" And the bear was so surprised and kerslostrated that he cried:

"Wow! Ouch! Oh, lollypops! Oh, sweet spirits of nitre!" And away he ran through the woods to hold his nose in a soft bank of mud, for he thought a bee had stung him. And so he didn't bite Uncle Wiggily after all.

"Well, I guess I can play marbles nearly as well as I used to," laughed the bunny uncle when Johnnie came back with the tall silk hat.

And when Mr. Longears told the boy squirrel about shooting the bear on the nose, Johnnie laughed and said he could have done no better himself.

So everything came out all right, you see, and if the butterfly doesn't try to stand on its head and tickle the June bug under the chin, I'll tell you next about Uncle Wiggily and Billie's top.

STORY XXII

UNCLE WIGGILY AND BILLIE'S TOP

Uncle Wiggily Longears, the nice rabbit gentleman, was sitting on the front porch of his hollow stump bungalow one day, when along came Billie Bushytail, the little squirrel boy.

"Hello, Billie!" called the bunny gentleman, cheerful-like and happy, for his rheumatism did not hurt him much that day. "Hello, Billie."

"Hello, Uncle Wiggily," answered the chattery squirrel chap. Then he came up and sat down on the porch, but he seemed so quiet and thoughtful that Uncle Wiggily asked:

"Is anything the matter, Billie?"

"No—well—that is, nothing much," said the squirrel boy slowly, "but I'd like to ask you what you'd buy if you had five cents, Uncle Wiggily."

"What would I buy if I had five cents, Billie? Well now, let me see. I think I'd buy two postage stamps and a funny postcard and write some letters to my friends. What would you buy, Billie?"

"I'd buy a spinning top, Uncle Wiggily," said the little squirrel boy, very quickly. "Only, you see, I haven't any five cents. You have, though, haven't you Uncle Wiggily? Eh?"

"Why, yes, Billie, I think so," and the old gentleman rabbit put his paw in his pocket to make sure.

"This is a funny world," said Billie with a long, sorrowful sigh. "Here you are with five cents and you don't want a top, and here I am without five cents and I do want a spinning top. Oh, dear!"

"Ha! Ha! Ha!" laughed Uncle Wiggily in his most jolly fashion. "I see what you mean, Billie. Now you just come along with me," and Uncle Wiggily picked up off the porch his red, white and blue striped barber-pole rheumatism crutch that Nurse Jane had gnawed for him out of a cornstalk.

"Where are we going?" asked Billie, sort of hopeful-like and expectant.

"I'm going to the top store to buy a spinning top," answered bunny uncle. "If you think I ought to have one, why I'll get it."

"Oh, all right," said Billie, sort of funny-like. "Do you know how to spin a top, Uncle Wiggily?"

"Well, I used to when I was a young rabbit, and I guess I can remember a little about it. Come along and help me pick out a nice one."

So the bunny uncle and the squirrel boy went on and on through the woods to the top store kept by Mrs. Spin Spider, who had a little toy shop in which she worked when she was not spinning silk for the animal ladies' dresses.

"One of your best tops for myself, if you please," said Uncle Wiggily, as he and Billie went into the toy store. Mrs. Spin Spider put a number of tops on the counter.

"That's the kind you want!" cried Billie, as he saw a big red one, and pointed his paw at it.

"Try it and see how it spins," said the bunny man.

Billie wound the string on the top, and then, giving it a throw, while he kept hold of one end of the cord, he made the top spin as fast as anything on the floor of the store. Around and around whizzed the red top, like the electric fan on Uncle Wiggily's airship.

"Is that a good top for me, Billie?" asked Mr. Longears.

"A very good top," said the squirrel boy. "Fine!"

"Then I'll take it," said Uncle Wiggily, and he paid for it and walked out, Billie following.

If the little chattery squirrel chap was disappointed at not getting a top for himself, he said nothing about it, which was very brave and good, I think. He just walked along until they came to a nice, smooth-dirt place in the woods, and then Uncle Wiggily said:

"Let me see you spin my top, Billie. I want to watch you and see how it's done—how you wind the string on, how you throw it down to the ground and all that. You just give me some lessons in top-spinning, please."

"I will," said Billie. So he wound the string on the top again and soon it was spinning as fast as anything on the hard ground in the woods.

"Do you want me to show you how to pick up a top, and let it spin on your paw?" asked Billie, of Uncle Wiggily.

"Yes, show me all the tricks there are," said the bunny gentleman.

So, while the top was spinning very fast, Billie picked it up, and, holding it on his paw, quickly put it over on Uncle Wiggily's paw.

"Ouch! It tickles!" cried the bunny uncle, sort of giggling like.

"Yes, a little," laughed Billie, "but I don't mind that. Now I'll show you how to pick it up."

Once more he spun the top, and he was just going to pick it up when, all of a sudden, a growling voice cried:

"Ah, ha! Again I am in luck! A rabbit and a squirrel! Let me see; which shall I take first?" And out from behind a stump popped a big bear. It was the same one that Uncle Wiggily had hit on the nose with Johnnie's marble, about a week before.

"Oh, my!" said the bunny man.

"Oh, dear!" chattered Billie.

"Surprised to see me, aren't you?" asked the bear sticking out his tongue.

"A little," answered Uncle Wiggily, "but I guess we'd better be getting along Billie. Pick up my top and come along."

"Oh, oh! Not so fast!" growled the bear. "I shall want you to stay with me. You'll be going off with me to my den, pretty soon. Don't be in a hurry," and, putting out his claws, he grabbed hold of Uncle Wiggily and Billie. They tried to get away, but could not, and the bear was just going to carry them off, when he saw the spinning top whizzing on the ground.

"What's that red thing?" he asked.

"A top Billie just picked out for me," said Uncle Wiggily.

"Would you like to have it spin on your paw?" asked Billie, blinking his eyes at Uncle Wiggily, funny-like.

"Oh, I might as well, before I carry you off to my den," said the bear, sort of careless-like and indifferent. "Spin the top on my paw."

So Billie picked up the spinning top and put it on the bear's broad, flat paw. And, no sooner was it there, whizzing around, than the bear cried:

"Ouch! Oh, dear! How it tickles. Ha! Ha! Ha! Ho! Ho! Ho! It makes me laugh. It makes me laugh. It makes me giggle! Ouch! Oh, dear!"

And then he laughed so hard that he dropped the top and turned a somersault, and away he ran through the woods, leaving Billie and Uncle Wiggily safe there alone.

"We came out of that very well," said the bunny uncle as the bear ran far away.

"Yes, indeed, and here is your top," spoke Billie, picking it up off the ground where the bear had dropped it.

"My top? No that's yours," said the bunny gentleman. "I meant it for you all the while."

"Oh, did you? Thank you so much!" cried happy Billie, and then he ran off to spin his red top, while Mr. Longears went back to his bungalow.

And if the sofa pillow doesn't leak its feathers all over, and make the room look like a bird's nest at a moving picture picnic, I'll tell you in the next story about Uncle Wiggily and the sunbeam.

STORY XXIII

UNCLE WIGGILY AND THE SUNBEAM

Uncle Wiggily Longears, the nice rabbit gentleman, was walking along in the woods one day, sort of hopping and leaning on his red, white and blue striped rheumatism crutch, and he was wondering whether or not he would have an adventure, when, all at once, he heard a little voice crying:

"Oh, dear! I never can get up! I never can get up! Oh, dear!"

"Ha! that sounds like some one who can't get out of bed," exclaimed the bunny uncle. "I wonder who it can be? Perhaps I can help them."

So he looked carefully around, but he saw no one, and he was just about to hop along, thinking perhaps he had made a mistake, and had not heard anything after all, when, suddenly, the voice sounded again, and called out:

"Oh, I can't get up! I can't get up! Can't you shine on me this way?"

"No, I am sorry to say I cannot," answered another voice. "But try to push your way through, and then I can shine on you, and make you grow."

There was silence for a minute, and then the first voice said again:

"Oh, it's no use! I can't push the stone from over my head. Oh, such trouble as I have!"

"Trouble, eh?" cried Uncle Wiggily. "Here is where I come in. Who are you, and what is the trouble?" he asked, looking all around, and seeing nothing but the shining sun.

"Here I am, down in the ground near your left hind leg," was the answer. "I am a woodland flower and I have just started to grow. But when I tried to put my head up out of the ground, to get air, and drink the rain water, I find I cannot do it. A big stone is in the way, right over my head, and I cannot push it aside to get up. Oh, dear!" sighed the Woodland flower.

"Oh, don't worry about that!" cried Uncle Wiggily, in his jolly voice. "I'll lift the stone off your head for you," and he did, just as he once had helped a Jack-in-the-pulpit flower to grow up, as I have told you in another story. Under the stone were two little pale green leaves on a stem that was just cracking its way up through the brown earth.

"There you are!" cried the bunny uncle. "But you don't look much like a flower."

"Oh! I have only just begun to grow," was the answer. "And I never would have been a flower if you had not taken the stone from me. You see, when I was a baby flower, or seed, I was covered up in my warm bed of earth. Then came the cold winter, and I went to sleep. When spring came I awakened and began to grow, but in the meanwhile this stone was put over me. I don't know by whom. But it held me down.

"But now I am free, and my pale green leaves will turn to dark green, and soon I will blossom out into a flower."

"How will all that happen?" Uncle Wiggily asked.

"When the sunbeam shines on me," answered the blossom. "That is why I wanted to get above the stone—so the sunbeam could shine on me and warm me."

"And I will begin to do it right now!" exclaimed the sunbeam, who had been playing about on the leaves of the trees, waiting for a chance to shine on the green plant and turn it into a beautiful flower. "Thank you, Uncle Wiggily, for taking the stone off the leaves so I could shine on them," went on the sunbeam, who had known Uncle

Wiggily for some time. "Though I am strong I am not strong enough to lift stones, nor was the flower. But now I can do my work. I thank you, and I hope I may do you a favor some time."

"Thank you," Uncle Wiggily said, with a low bow, raising his tall silk hat. "I suppose you sunbeams are kept very busy shining on, and warming, all the plants and trees in the woods?"

"Yes, indeed!" answered the yellow sunbeam, who was a long, straight chap. "We have lots of work to do, but we are never too busy to shine for our friends."

Then the sunbeam played about the little green plant, turning the pale leaves a darker color and swelling out the tiny buds. Uncle Wiggily walked on through the woods, glad that he had had even this little adventure.

It was a day or so after this that the bunny uncle went to the store for Nurse Jane Fuzzy Wuzzy, the muskrat lady, who kept his hollow stump bungalow so nice and tidy.

"I want a loaf of bread, a yeast cake and three pounds of sugar," said Nurse Jane.

"It will give me great pleasure to get them for you," answered the rabbit gentleman politely. On his way home from the store with the sugar, bread and yeast cake, Uncle Wiggily thought he would hop past the place where he had lifted the stone off the head of the plant, to see how it was growing. And, as he stood there, looking at the flower, which was much taller than when the bunny uncle had last seen it, all of a sudden there was a rustling in the bushes, and out jumped a bad old fox.

"Ah, ha!" barked the fox, like a dog. "You are just the one I want to see!"

"You want to see me?" exclaimed Uncle Wiggily. "I think you must be mistaken," he went on politely.

"Oh, no, not at all!" barked the fox. "You have there some sugar, some bread and a yeast cake; have you not?"

"I have," answered Uncle Wiggily.

"Well, then, you may give me the bread and sugar and after I eat them I will start in on you. I will take you off to my den, to my dear little foxes. Eight, Nine and Ten. They have numbers instead of names, you see."

"But I don't want to give you Nurse Jane's sugar and bread, and go with you to your den," said the rabbit gentleman. "I don't want to! I don't like it!"

"You can't always do as you like," barked the fox. "Quick now—the sugar and bread!"

"What about the yeast cake?" asked Uncle Wiggily, as he held it out, all wrapped in shiny tinfoil, like a looking-glass. "What about the yeast cake?"

"Oh, throw it away!" growled the fox.

"No, don't you do it!" whispered a voice in Uncle Wiggily's ear, and there was the sunbeam he had met the other day. "Hold out the yeast cake and I will shine on it very brightly, and then I'll slant, or bounce off from it, into the eyes of the fox," said the sunbeam. "And when I shine in his eyes I'll tickle him, and he'll sneeze, and you can run away."

So Uncle Wiggily held out the bright yeast cake. Quick as a flash the sunbeam glittered on it, and then reflected itself into the eyes of the fox.

"Ker-chool!" he sneezed. "Ker-chooaker-choo!" and tears came into the fox's eyes, so he could not see Uncle Wiggily, who, after thanking the sunbeam, hurried safely back to his bungalow with the things for Nurse Jane.

So the fox got nothing at all but a sneeze, you see, and when he had cleared the tears out of his eyes Uncle Wiggily was gone. So the sunbeam did the bunny gentleman a favor after all, and if the coal man doesn't put oranges in our cellar, in mistake for apples when he brings a barrel of wood, I'll tell you next about Uncle Wiggily and the puff ball.

STORY XXIV

UNCLE WIGGILY AND THE PUFF BALL

"Are you going for a walk to-day, as you nearly always do, Uncle Wiggily?" asked Nurse Jane Fuzzy, the muskrat lady housekeeper, of the rabbit gentleman, as he got up from the breakfast table in the hollow stump bungalow one morning.

"Why, yes, Janie, I am going for a walk in the woods very soon," answered Uncle Wiggily. "Is there anything I can do for you?"

"There is," said the muskrat lady. "Something for yourself, also."

"What is it?" Uncle Wiggily wanted to know, sort of making his pink nose turn orange color by looking up at the sun and sneezing. "What is it that I can do for myself as well as for you, Janie?"

"Cream puffs," answered Miss Fuzzy Wuzzy.

"Cream puffs?" cried the bunny uncle, hardly knowing whether his housekeeper was fooling or in earnest.

"Yes, I want some cream puffs for supper, and if you stop at the baker's and get them you will be doing yourself a favor as well as me, for we will both eat them."

"Right gladly will I do it," Uncle Wiggily made answer. "Cream puffs I shall bring from the baker's," and then, whistling a funny little tune, away he hopped to the woods.

It did not take him long to get to the place where the baker had his shop. And in a few minutes Uncle Wiggily was on his way back with some delicious cream puffs in a basket.

"I'll take them home to Nurse Jane for supper," thought the bunny uncle, "and then I can keep on with my walk, looking for an adventure."

You know what cream puffs are, I dare say. They are little, round, puffy balls made of something like piecrust, and they are hollow. The inside is filled with something like corn-starch pudding, only nicer.

Uncle Wiggily was going along with the cream puffs in his basket when, coming to a nice place in the woods, where the sun shone on a green, mossy log, the bunny uncle said:

"I will sit down here a minute and rest."

So he did, but he rested longer than he meant to, for, before he knew it, he fell asleep. And while he slept, along came a bad old weasel, who is as sly as a fox. And the weasel, smelling the cream puffs in the basket, slyly lifted the cover and took every one out, eating them one after the other.

"Now to play a trick on Uncle Wiggily," said the weasel in a whisper, for the bunny uncle was still sleeping. So the bad creature found a lot of puff balls in the woods, and put them in the basket in place of the cream puffs.

Puff balls grow on little plants. They are brown and round and hollow, and, so far, they are like cream puffs, except that inside they have a brown, fluffy powder that flies all over when you break the puff ball. And, if you are not careful, it gets in your eyes and nose and makes you sneeze.

"I should like to see what Uncle Wiggily and Nurse Jane do when they open the basket, and find puff balls instead of cream puffs," snickered the weasel as he went off, licking his chops, where the cornstarch pudding stuff was stuck on his whiskers. "It will be a great joke on them!"

But let us see what happens.

Uncle Wiggily awakened from his sleep in the woods, and started off toward his hollow stump bungalow.

"I declare!" he cried. "That sleep made me hungry. I shall be glad to eat some of the cream puffs I have in my basket."

"What's that?" asked a sharp voice in the bushes. "What did you say you had in the basket?"

"Cream puffs," answered Uncle Wiggily, without thinking, and then, all of a sudden, out jumped the bad old skillery-scalery alligator with the humps on his tail.

"Ha! Cream puffs!" cried the 'gator, as I call him for short, though he was rather long. "Cream puffs! If there is one thing I like more than another it is cream puffs! It is lucky you brought them with you, or I would have nothing for dessert when I have you for supper."

"Are you—are you going to have me for supper?" asked Uncle Wiggily, sort of anxious like.

"I am!" cried the alligator, positively. "But I will eat the dessert first. Give me those cream puffs!" he cried and he made a grab for the bunny's basket, and, reaching in, scooped out the puff balls, thinking they were cream puffs. The 'gator, without looking, took one bite and a chew and then— —

"Oh, my! Ker-sneezio! Ker-snitzio! Ker-choo!" he sneezed as the powder from the puff balls went up his nose and into his eyes. "Oh, what funny cream puffs! Wow!" And, not stopping to so much as nibble at Uncle Wiggily, away ran the alligator to get a drink of lemonade.

"Ker-sneezio! Ker-snitzio! Ker-choo!" he sneezed as the powder from the puff balls went up his nose and into his eyes.

So you see, after all, the weasel's trick saved Uncle Wiggily, who soon went back to the store for more cream puffs—real ones this time, and he got safely home with them.

And nothing else happened that day. But if the trolley car stops running down the street to play with the jitney bus, so the pussy cat can have a ride when it wants to go shopping in the three and four-cent store, I'll tell you next about Uncle Wiggily and the May flowers.

STORY XXV

UNCLE WIGGILY AND THE MAY FLOWERS

"Rat-a-tat!" came a knock on the door of the hollow stump bungalow, where Uncle Wiggily Longears, the rabbit gentleman, lived in the woods with Nurse Jane Fuzzy Wuzzy, his muskrat lady housekeeper.

"My! Some one is calling early to-day!" said the bunny uncle.

"Sit still and eat your breakfast," spoke Nurse Jane. "I'll see who it is."

When she opened the door there stood Jimmie Wibblewobble, the boy duck.

"Why where are you going so early this morning, Jimmie?" asked Uncle Wiggily.

"I'm going to school," answered the Wibblewobble chap, who was named that because his tail did wibble and wobble from side to side when he walked.

"Aren't you a bit early?" asked Mr. Longears.

"I came early to get you," said Jimmie. "Will you come for a walk with me, Uncle Wiggily? We can walk toward the hollow stump school, where the lady mouse teaches us our lessons."

"Why, it's so very early," Uncle Wiggily went on. "I have hardly had my breakfast. Why so early, Jimmie?"

The duck boy whispered in Uncle Wiggily's ear:

"I want to go early so I can gather some May flowers for the teacher. This is the first day of May, you know, and the flowers that have been wet by the April showers ought to be blossoming now."

"So they had!" cried Uncle Wiggily. "I'll hurry with my breakfast, Jimmie, and we'll go gathering May flowers in the woods."

Soon the bunny uncle and the boy duck were walking along where the green trees grew up out of the carpet of soft green moss.

"Oh, here are some yellow violets!" cried Jimmie, as he saw some near an old stump.

"Yes, and I see some white ones!" cried the bunny uncle, as he picked them, while Jimmie plucked the yellow violets with his strong bill, which was also yellow in color.

Then they went on a little farther and saw some bluebells growing, and the bluebell flowers were tinkling a pretty little tinkle tune.

The bluebells even kept on tinkling after Jimmie had picked them for his bouquet. The boy duck waddled on a little farther and all of a sudden, he cried:

"Oh, what a funny flower this is, Uncle Wiggily. It's just like the little ice cream cones that come on Christmas trees, only it's covered with a flap, like a leaf, and under the flap is a little green thing, standing up. What is it?"

"That is a Jack-in-the-pulpit," answered the bunny uncle, "and the Jack is the funny green thing. Jack preaches sermons to the other flowers, telling them how to be beautiful and make sweet perfume."

"I'm going to put a Jack in the bouquet for the lady mouse teacher," said Jimmie, and he did.

Then he and Uncle Wiggily went farther and farther on in the woods, picking May flowers, and they were almost at the hollow stump school when, all at once, from behind a big stone popped the bad ear-scratching cat.

"Ah, ha!" howled the cat. "I am just in time I see. I haven't scratched any ears in ever and ever so long. And you have such nice, big ears, Uncle Wiggily, that it is a real pleasure to scratch them!"

"Do you mean it is a pleasure for me, or for you?" asked the bunny uncle, softly like.

"For me, of course!" meaouwed the cat. "Get ready now for the ear-scratching! Here I come!"

"Oh, please don't scratch my ears!" begged Uncle Wiggily. "Please don't!"

"Yes, I shall!" said the bad cat, stretching out his claws.

"Would you mind scratching my ears, instead of Uncle Wiggily's?" asked Jimmie. "I'll let you scratch mine all you want to."

"I don't want to," spoke the cat. "Your ears are so small that it is no pleasure for me to scratch them—none at all."

"It was very kind of you to offer your ears in place of mine," said Uncle Wiggily to the duck boy. "But I can't let you do that. Go on, bad cat, if you are going to scratch my ears, please do it and have it over with."

"All right!" snarled the cat. "I'll scratch your ears!" She was just going to do it, when Jimmie suddenly picked up a new flower, and holding it toward the cat cried:

"No, you can't scratch Uncle Wiggily's ears! This is a dog-tooth violet I have just picked, and if you harm Uncle Wiggily I'll make the dog-tooth violet bite you!"

And then the big violet went: "Bow! Wow! Wow!" just like a dog, and the cat thinking a dog was after him, meaouwed:

"Oh, my! Oh, dear! This is no place for me!" and away he ran, not scratching Uncle Wiggily at all.

Then Jimmie put the dog-tooth violet (which did not bark any more) in his bouquet and the lady mouse teacher liked the May flowers very much. Uncle Wiggily took his flowers to Nurse Jane.

And if the umbrella doesn't turn inside out, so its ribs get all wet and sneeze the handle off, I'll tell you next about Uncle Wiggily and the beech tree.

STORY XXVI

UNCLE WIGGILY AND THE BEECH TREE

"Will you go to the store for me, Uncle Wiggily?" asked Nurse Jane Fuzzy Wuzzy, the muskrat lady housekeeper, of the rabbit gentleman one day, as he sat out on the porch of his hollow stump bungalow in the woods.

"Indeed I will, Miss Fuzzy Wuzzy," said Mr. Longears, most politely. "What is it you want?"

"A loaf of bread and a pound of sugar," she answered, and Uncle Wiggily started off.

"Better take your umbrella," Nurse Jane called after him. "All the April showers are not yet over, even if it is May."

So the rabbit gentleman took his umbrella.

On his way to the store through the woods, the bunny uncle came to a big beech tree, which had nice, shiny white bark on it, and, to his surprise the rabbit gentleman saw a big black bear, standing up on his hind legs and scratching at the tree bark as hard as he could.

"Ha! That is not the right thing to do," said Uncle Wiggily to himself. "If that bear scratches too much of the bark from the tree the tree will die, for the bark of a tree is just like my skin is to me. I must drive the bear away."

The bear, scratching the bark with his sharp claws, stood with his back to Uncle Wiggily, and the rabbit gentleman thought he could scare the big creature away.

So Uncle Wiggily picked up a stone, and throwing it at the bear, hit him on the back, where the skin was so thick it hurt hardly at all.

124

And as soon as he had thrown the stone Uncle Wiggily in his loudest voice shouted:

"Bang! Bang! Bungity-bang-bung!"

"Oh, my goodness!" cried the bear, not turning around. "The hunter man with his gun must be after me. He has shot me once, but the bullet did not hurt. I had better run away before he shoots me again!"

And the bear ran away, never once looking around, for he thought the stone Mr. Longears threw was a bullet from a gun, you see, and he thought when Uncle Wiggily said "Bang!" that it was a gun going off. So the bunny gentleman scared the bear away.

"Thank you, Uncle Wiggily," said the beech tree. "You saved my life by not letting the bear scratch off all my bark."

"I am glad I did," spoke the rabbit, making a polite bow with his tall silk hat, for Mr. Longears was polite, even to a tree.

"The bear would not stop scratching my bark when I asked him to," went on the beech tree, "so I am glad you came along, and scared him. You did me a great favor and I will do you one if I ever can."

"Thank you," spoke Uncle Wiggily, and then he hopped on to the store to get the loaf of bread and the pound of sugar for Nurse Jane.

It was on the way back from the store that an adventure happened to Uncle Wiggily. He came to the place where his friend the beech tree was standing up in the woods, and a balsam tree, next door to it, was putting some salve, or balsam, on the places where the bear had scratched off the bark, to make the cuts heal.

Then, all of a sudden, out from behind a bush jumped the same bad bear that had done the scratching.

"Ah, ha!" growled the bear, as soon as he saw Uncle Wiggily, "you can't fool me again, making believe a stone is a bullet, and that your 'Bang!' is a gun! You can't fool me! I know all about the trick you played on me. A little bird, sitting up in a tree, saw it and told me!"

"Well," said Uncle Wiggily slowly, "I'm sorry I had to fool you, but it was all for the best. I wanted to save the beech tree."

"Oh, I don't care!" cried the bear, saucy like and impolitely. "I'm going to scratch as much as I like!"

"My goodness! You're almost as bad as the ear-scratching cat!" said Uncle Wiggily. "I guess I'd better run home to my hollow stump bungalow."

"No, you don't!" cried the bear, and, reaching out his claws, he caught hold of Uncle Wiggily, who, with his umbrella, and the bread and sugar, was standing under the beech tree. "You can't get away from me like that," and the bear held tightly to the bunny uncle.

"Oh, dear! What are you going to do to me?" asked the rabbit gentleman.

"First, I'll bite you," said the bear. "No, I guess I'll first scratch you. No, I won't either. I'll scrite you; that's what I'll do. I'll scrite you!"

"What's scrite?" asked Uncle Wiggily, curious like.

"It's a scratch and a bite made into one," said the bear, "and now I'm going to do it."

"Oh, ho! No, you aren't!" suddenly cried the beech tree, who had been thinking of a way to save Uncle Wiggily. "No, you don't scrite my friend!" And with that the brave tree gave itself a shiver and shake, and shook down on the bear a lot of sharp, three-cornered beech nuts. They fell on the bear's soft and tender nose and the sharp edges hurt him so that he cried:

126

"Wow! Ouch! I guess I made a mistake! I must run away!"

And away he ran from the shower of sharp beech nuts which didn't hurt Uncle Wiggily at all because he raised his umbrella and kept them off. Then he thanked the tree for having saved him from the bear and went safely home. And if the cow bell doesn't moo in its sleep, and wake up the milkman before it's time to bring the molasses for breakfast, I'll tell you next about Uncle Wiggily and the bitter medicine.

STORY XXVII

UNCLE WIGGILY AND THE BITTER MEDICINE

"How is Jackie this morning, Mrs. Bow Wow?" asked Uncle Wiggily Longears, the rabbit gentleman, one day, as he stopped at the kennel where the dog lady lived with her two little boys, Jackie and Peetie Bow Wow, the puppies. "How is Jackie?"

"Jackie is not so well, I'm sorry to say," answered Mrs. Bow Wow, as she looked carefully along the back fence to see if there were any bad cats there who might meaouw, and try to scratch the puppies.

"Not so well? I am sorry to hear that," spoke the bunny uncle. "What's seems to be the matter?"

"Oh, you know Jackie and Peetie both had the measles," went on Mrs. Bow Wow. "They seemed to get over them nicely, at least Peetie did, but then Jackie caught the epizootic, and he has to stay in bed a week longer, and take bitter medicine."

"Bitter medicine, eh?" exclaimed Uncle Wiggily. "I am sorry to hear that, for I don't like bitter medicine myself."

"Neither does Jackie," continued Mrs. Bow Wow. "In fact, he really doesn't know whether he likes this bitter medicine or not."

"Why, not?" asked the rabbit gentleman.

"Because we can't get him to take a drop," said the puppy dog boy's mother. "Not a drop will he take, though I have fixed it up for him with orange juice and sugar and even put it in a lollypop. But he won't take it, and Dr. Possum says he won't get well unless he takes the bitter medicine."

"Well, Dr. Possum ought to know," said Uncle Wiggily. "But why don't you ask him a good way to give the medicine to Jackie?"

"That's what I'm waiting out here for now," said Mrs. Bow Wow. "I want to catch Dr. Possum when he comes past, and ask him to come in and give Jackie the medicine. The poor boy really needs it to make him well."

"Of course he does," agreed Uncle Wiggily. "And while you are waiting for Dr. Possum I'll see what I can do."

"What are you going to do?" asked Mrs. Bow Wow, as the bunny uncle started for the dog kennel.

"I'm going to try to make Jackie take his bitter medicine. You just stay out here a little while."

"Well, I hope you do it, but I'm afraid you won't," spoke Mrs. Bow Wow with a sigh. "I've tried all the ways I know. I was just going, as you came along, to get a toy balloon, blow it up, and put the medicine inside. Then I was going to let Jackie burst it by sticking a pin in it. And I thought when the balloon exploded the medicine might be blown down his throat."

"Oh, well, I think I have a better way than that," said Uncle Wiggily with a laugh. He went in where Jackie, who had the measles-epizootic, was in bed. "Good morning, Jackie," said the bunny uncle. "How are you?"

"Not very well," answered Jackie, the puppy dog boy. "But I'm glad to see you. I'm not going to take the bitter medicine even for you, though, Uncle Wiggily."

"Ho! Ho! Ho! Just you wait until you're asked!" cried Mr. Longears in his most jolly voice. "Now let me have a look at that bitter medicine which is making so much trouble. Where is it?"

"In that cup on the chair," and Jackie pointed to it near his bed.

"I see," said Uncle Wiggily, looking at it. "Now, Jackie, I'm a good friend of yours, and you wouldn't mind just holding this cup of bitter medicine in your paw, would you, to please me?"

"Oh, I'll do that for you, Uncle Wiggily, but I'll not take it," Jackie said.

"Never mind about that," laughed the bunny uncle. "Just hold the medicine in your paw, so," and Jackie did as he was told. "Now, would you mind holding it up to your lips, as if you were going to make believe take it?" asked Uncle Wiggily. "Mind you, don't you dare take a drop of it. Just hold the cup to your lips, but don't swallow any."

"Why do you want me to do that?" asked Jackie, as he did what Uncle Wiggily asked.

"Because I want to draw a picture of you making believe take bitter medicine," said the bunny, as he took out pencil and paper. "I'll show it to any other of my little animal friends, who may not like their medicine, and I'll say to them: 'See how brave Jackie is to take his bitter medicine.' Of course, I won't tell them you really were afraid to take it," and without saying any more Uncle Wiggily began to draw the puppy dog boy's picture on the paper.

"Hold the cup a little nearer to your lips, and tip it up a bit, Jackie," said the bunny man. "But, mind you, don't swallow a drop. That's it, higher up! Tip it more. I want the picture to look natural."

Jackie tipped the cup higher, holding it close to his mouth, and threw back his head, and then Uncle Wiggily suddenly cried: "Ouch!" And Jackie was so surprised that he opened his mouth and before he knew it he had swallowed the bitter medicine!

Jackie was so surprised that he opened his mouth.

"Oh, why I took it!" he cried. "It went down my throat! And it wasn't so bad, after all."

"I thought it wouldn't be," spoke Uncle Wiggily, as he finished the picture of Jackie, and now he could really say it showed the doggie boy actually taking the medicine, for Jackie did take it.

So Dr. Possum didn't have to come in to see Jackie after all to make him swallow the bitter stuff, and the little chap was soon all well again. And if the clothesline doesn't try to jump rope with the Jack in the Box, and upset the washtub, I'll tell you next about Uncle Wiggily and the pine cones.

STORY XXVIII

UNCLE WIGGILY AND THE PINE CONES

Uncle Wiggily Longears, the nice rabbit gentleman, was out walking in the woods one day when he felt rather tired. He had been looking all around for an adventure, which was something he liked to have happen to him, but he had seen nothing like one so far.

"And I don't want to go back to my hollow stump bungalow without having had an adventure to tell Nurse Jane Fuzzy Wuzzy about," said Mr. Longears.

But, as I said, the rabbit gentleman was feeling rather tired, and, seeing a nice log covered with a cushion of green moss, he sat down on that to rest.

"Perhaps an adventure will happen to me here," thought the bunny uncle as he leaned back against a pine tree to rest.

It was nice and warm in the woods, and, with the sun shining down upon him, Uncle Wiggily soon dozed off in a little sleep. But when he awakened still no adventure had happened to him.

"Well, I guess I must travel on," he said, and he started to get up, but he could not. He could not move his back away from the pine tree against which he had leaned to rest.

"Oh, dear! what has happened," cried the bunny uncle. "I am stuck fast! I can't get away! Oh, dear!"

At first he thought perhaps the skillery-scalery alligator with the humps on his tail had come softly up behind him as he slept and had him in his claws. But, by sort of looking around backward, Mr. Longears could see no one—not even a fox.

133

"But what is it holding me?" he cried, as he tried again and again to get loose, but could not.

"I am sorry to say I am holding you!" spoke a voice up over Uncle Wiggily's head. "I am holding you fast!"

"Who are you, if you please?" asked the rabbit gentleman.

"I am the pine tree against which you leaned your back. And on my bark was a lot of sticky pine gum. It is that which is holding you fast," the tree answered.

"Why—why, it's just like sticky flypaper, isn't it?" asked Uncle Wiggily, trying again to get loose, but not doing so. "And it is just like the time you held the bear fast for me."

"Yes, it is; and flypaper is made from my sticky pine gum," said the tree. "I am so sorry you are stuck, but I did not see you lean back against me until it was too late. And now I can't get you loose, for my limbs are so high over your head that I can not reach them down to you. Try to get loose yourself."

"I will," said Uncle Wiggily, and he did, but he could not get loose, though he almost pulled out all his fur. So he cried:

"Help! Help! Help!"

Then, all of a sudden, along through the woods came Neddie Stubtail, the little bear-boy, and Neddie had some butter, which he had just bought at the store for his mother.

"Oh!" cried the pine tree. "If you will rub some butter on my sticky gum, it will loosen and melt it, so Uncle Wiggily will not be stuck any more."

Neddie did so, and soon the bunny uncle was free.

"Oh, I can't tell you how sorry I am," said the pine tree. "I am a horrid creature, of no use in this world, Uncle Wiggily! Other trees have nice fruit or nuts or flowers on them, but all I have is sticky gum, or brown, rough ugly pine cones. Oh, dear! I am of no use in the world!"

"Oh, yes you are!" said Uncle Wiggily, kindly. "As for having stuck me fast, that was my own fault. I should have looked before I leaned back. And, as for your pine cones, I dare say they are very useful."

"No, they are not!" said the tree sadly. "If they were only ice cream cones they might be some good. Oh, I wish I were a peach tree, or a rose bush!"

"Never mind," spoke Uncle Wiggily, "I like your pine cones, and I am going to take some home with me, and, when I next see you, I shall tell you how useful they were. Don't feel so badly."

So Uncle Wiggily gathered a number of the pine cones, which are really the big, dried seeds of the pine tree, and the bunny uncle took them to his bungalow with him.

A few days later he was in the woods again and stopped near the pine tree, which was sighing and wishing it were an umbrella plant or a gold fish.

"Hush!" cried Uncle Wiggily. "You must try to do the best you can for what you are! And I have come to tell you how useful your pine cones were."

"Really?" asked the tree, in great surprise. "Really?"

"Really and truly," answered Uncle Wiggily. "With some of your cones Nurse Jane started her kitchen fire when all the wood was wet. With others I built a little play house, and amused Lulu Wibblewobble, the duck girl, when she had the toothache. And other cones I threw at a big bear that was chasing me. I hit him on the nose with them, and he was glad enough to run away. So you see how useful you are, pine tree!"

"Oh, I am so glad," said the tree. "I guess it is better to be just what you are, and do the best you can," and Uncle Wiggily said it was.

And, if the roof of our house doesn't come down stairs to play with the kitchen floor and let the rain in on the gold fish, I'll tell you next about Uncle Wiggily and his torn coat.

STORY XXIX

UNCLE WIGGILY AND HIS TORN COAT

"Do you think I look all right?" asked Uncle Wiggily Longears, the rabbit gentleman, of Nurse Jane Fuzzy Wuzzy, his muskrat lady housekeeper. He was standing in front of her, turning slowly about, and he had on a new coat. For now that Summer was near the bunny uncle had laid aside his heavy fur coat and was wearing a lighter one.

"Yes, you do look very nice," Nurse Jane said, tying her tail in a knot so Uncle Wiggily would not step on it as he turned around.

"Nice enough to go to Grandfather Goosey Gander's party?" asked the rabbit gentleman.

"Oh, yes, indeed!" exclaimed Nurse Jane. "I didn't know Grandpa Goosey was to give a party, but, if he is, you certainly look well enough to go with your new coat. Of course, it might be better if it had some lace insertion around the button holes, or a bit of ruching, with oyster shell trimming sewed down the back, but—"

"Oh, no, indeed!" laughed the bunny uncle. "If it had those things on it would be a coat for a lady. I like mine plainer."

"Well, take care of yourself," called Nurse Jane after him as he hopped off over the fields and through the woods to the house where Grandfather Goosey Gander lived.

"Now, I must be very careful not to get my new coat dirty, or I won't look nice at the party," the old rabbit gentleman was saying to himself as he hopped along. "I must be very careful indeed."

He went along as carefully as he could, but, just as he was going down a little hill, under the trees, he came to a place which was so slippery that, before he knew it, all of a sudden Uncle Wiggily fell down and slid to the bottom of the hill.

"My goodness!" he cried, as he stood up after his slide. "I did not know there was snow or ice on that hill."

And when he looked there was not, but it was covered with long, thin pine needles, which are almost as slippery as glass. It was on these that the rabbit gentleman had slipped down hill.

"Well, there is no great harm done," said Uncle Wiggily to himself, as he found no bones broken. "I had a little slide, that's all. I must bring Sammie and Susie Littletail here some day, and let them slide on pine needle hill. Johnnie and Billie Bushytail, the two squirrels, would also like it, and so would Nannie and Billie Wagtail, my two goat friends."

Uncle Wiggily was about to go on to the party when, as he looked at his new coat he saw that it was all torn. In sliding down the slippery pine needle hill the coat had caught on sticks and stones and it had many holes torn in it, and it was also ripped here and there.

"Oh, dear me!" cried Uncle Wiggily. "Oh, sorrow! Oh, unhappiness! Now I'll have to go back to my hollow stump bungalow and put on my old coat that isn't torn. For I never can wear my new one to the party. That would never do! But the trouble is, if I go back home I'll be late! Oh, dear, what trouble I am in!"

Now was the time for some of Uncle Wiggily's friends to help him in his trouble, as he had often helped them. But, as he looked through the woods, he could not see even a little mouse, or so much as a grasshopper.

"The tailor bird would be just the one I'd like to see now," said the rabbit uncle. "She could mend my torn coat nicely." For tailor birds, yon know, can take a piece of grass, with their bill for a needle, and sew leaves together to make a nest, almost as well as your mother can mend a hole in your stocking.

But there was no tailor bird in the woods, and Uncle Wiggily did not know what to do.

"I certainly do not want to be late to Grandpa Goosey's party," said the bunny uncle, "nor do I want to go to it in a torn coat. Oh, dear!"

Just then he heard down on the ground near him, a little voice saying:

"Perhaps we could mend your coat for you, Uncle Wiggily."

"You. Who are you, and how can you mend my torn coat?" the bunny gentleman wanted to know.

"We are some little black ants," was the answer, "and with the pine needles lying on the ground—some of the same needles on which you slipped—we can sew up your coat, with long grass for thread."

"Oh, that will be fine, if you can do it," spoke the bunny uncle. "Can you?"

"We'll try," the ants said. Then, about fourteen thousand six hundred and twenty-two black ants took each a long, sharp pine needle, and threading it with grass, they began to sew up the rips and tears in Uncle Wiggily's coat. And in places where they could not easily sew they stuck the cloth together with sticky gum from the pine tree. So, though the pine tree was to blame, in a way, for Uncle Wiggily's fall, it also helped in the mending of his coat.

Soon the coat was almost as good as new and you could hardly tell where it was torn. And Uncle Wiggily, kindly thanking the ants, went on to Grandpa Goosey's party and had a fine time and also some ice cream.

And if the egg beater doesn't take all the raisins out of the rice pudding, so it looks like a cup of custard going to the moving pictures, the next story will be about Uncle Wiggily and the sycamore tree.

STORY XXX

UNCLE WIGGILY AND THE SYCAMORE TREE

"Oh, Uncle Wiggily, I'm going to a party! I'm going to a party!" cried Nannie Wagtail, the little goat girl, as she pranced up in front of the hollow stump bungalow where Mr. Longears, the rabbit gentleman, lived with Nurse Jane Fuzzy Wuzzy, the muskrat lady housekeeper.

"Going to a party? Say, that's just fine!" said the bunny gentleman. "I wish I were going to one."

"Why, you can come, too!" cried Nannie. "Jillie Longtail, the little mouse girl, is giving the party, and I know she will be glad to have you."

"Well, perhaps, I may stop in for a little while," said Mr. Longears, with a smile that made his pink nose twinkle like the frosting on a sponge cake. "But when is the party going to take place, Nannie?"

"Right away—I'm going there now; but I just stopped at your bungalow to show you my new shoes that Uncle Butter, the circus poster goat, bought for me. Aren't they nice?" And she stuck out her feet.

"Indeed, they are!" cried Uncle Wiggily, as he looked at the shiny black shoes which went on over Nannie's hoofs. "So the party is to-day, is it?",

"Right now," said Nannie. "Come on, Uncle Wiggily. Walk along with me and go in! They'll all be glad to see you!"

"Oh, but my dear child!" cried the bunny gentleman. "I haven't shaved my whiskers, my ears need brushing, and I would have to do lots of things to make myself look nice and ready for a party!"

"Oh, dear!" bleated Nannie Wagtail. "I did so want you to come with me!"

"Well, I'll walk as far as the Longtail mouse home,"' said the bunny uncle, "but I won't go in.

"Oh, maybe you will when you get there!" And Nannie laughed, for she knew Uncle Wiggily always did whatever the animal children wanted him to do.

So the bunny uncle and Nannie started off through the woods together, Nannie looking down at her new shoes every now and then.

"I'm going to dance at the party, Uncle Wiggily!" she said.

"I should think you would, Nannie, with those nice new shoes," spoke Mr. Longears. "What dance are you going to do?"

"Oh, the four-step and the fish hornpipe, I guess," answered Nannie, and then she suddenly cried:

"Oh, dear!"

"What's the matter now?" asked Uncle Wiggily. "Did you lose one of your new shoes?"

"No, but I splashed some mud on it," the little goat girl said. "I stepped in a mud puddle."

"Never mind, I'll wipe it off with a bit of soft green moss," answered Uncle Wiggily; and he did. So Nannie's shoes were all clean again.

On and on went the rabbit gentleman and the little goat girl, and they talked of what games the animal children would play at the Longtail mouse party, and what good things they would eat, and all like that.

All of a sudden, as Nannie was jumping over another little puddle of water, she cried out again:

"Oh, dear!"

"What's the matter now?" asked Uncle Wiggily. "Did some more mud splash on your new shoes, Nannie?"

"No, Uncle Wiggily, but a lot of the buttons came off. I guess they don't fasten buttons on new shoes very tight."

"I guess they don't," Uncle Wiggily said. "But still you have enough buttons left to keep the shoes on your feet. I guess you will be all right."

So Nannie walked on a little farther, with Uncle Wiggily resting his rheumatism, now and then, on the red, white and blue striped barber pole crutch that Nurse Jane had gnawed for him out of a cornstalk.

All of a sudden Nannie cried out again:

"Oh, dear! Oh, this is too bad!"

"What is?" asked Uncle Wiggily.

"Now all the buttons have come off my shoes!" said the little goat girl, sadly. "I don't see how I can go on to the party and dance, with no buttons on my shoes. They'll be slipping off all the while."

"So they will," spoke Uncle Wiggily. "Shoes without buttons are like lollypops without sticks, you can't do anything with them."

"But what am I going to do?" asked Nannie, while tears came into her eyes and splashed up on her horns. "I do want so much to go to that party."

"And I want you to," said Uncle Wiggily. "Let me think a minute."

So he thought and thought, and then he looked off through the woods and he saw a queer tree not far away. It was a sycamore tree, with broad white patches on the smooth bark, and hanging down from the branches were lots of round balls, just like shoe buttons, only they were a sort of brown instead of black. The balls were the seeds of the tree.

"Ha! The very thing!" cried the bunny uncle.

"What is?" asked Nannie.

"That sycamore, or button-ball tree," answered the rabbit gentleman. "I can get you some new shoe buttons off that, Nannie, and sew them on your shoes."

"Oh, if you can, that will be just fine!" cried the little goat girl. "For when the buttons came off my new shoes they flew every which way—I mean the buttons did—and I couldn't find a single one."

"Never mind," Uncle Wiggily kindly said. "I'll sew on some of the buttons from the sycamore tree, and everything will be all right."

With a thorn for a needle, and some long grasses for thread, Uncle Wiggily soon sewed the buttons from the sycamore, or button-ball, tree on Nannie's new shoes, using the very smallest ones, of course. Then Nannie put on her shoes again, having rested her feet on a velvet carpet of moss, while Uncle Wiggily was sewing, and together they went on to the Longtail mouse party.

"Oh, what nice shoes you have, Nannie!" cried Susie Littletail, the rabbit girl.

"And what lovely stylish buttons!" exclaimed Lulu Wibblewobble, the duck.

"Yes, Uncle Wiggily sewed them on for me," said Nannie.

"Oh, is Uncle Wiggily outside!" cried the little mousie girl. "He must come in to our party!"

"Of course!" cried all the other animal children. And so Uncle Wiggily, who had walked on past the house after leaving Nannie, had to come in anyhow, without his whiskers being trimmed, or his ears curled. And he was so jolly that every one had a good time and lots of ice cream cheese to eat, and they all thought Nannie's shoes, and the button-ball buttons, were just fine.

And if the ham sandwich doesn't tickle the cream puff under the chin and make it laugh so all the chocolate drops off the cocoanut pudding, I'll tell you next about Uncle Wiggily and the red spots.

STORY XXXI

UNCLE WIGGILY AND THE RED SPOTS

Uncle Wiggily Longears, the rabbit gentleman, was hopping along through the woods one fine day when he heard a little voice calling to him:

"Oh, Uncle Wiggily! Will you have a game of tag with me?"

At first the bunny uncle thought the voice might belong to a bad fox or a harum-scarum bear, but when he had peeked through the bushes he saw that it was Lulu Wibblewobble, the duck girl, who had called to him.

"Have a game of tag with you? Why, of course, I will!" laughed Uncle Wiggily. "That is, if you will kindly excuse my rheumatism, and the red, white and blue crutch which Nurse Jane Fuzzy Wuzzy, my muskrat lady housekeeper, gnawed for me out of a cornstalk."

"Of course, I'll excuse it, Uncle Wiggily," said Lulu. "Only please don't tag me with the end of your crutch, for it tickles me, and when I'm tickled I have to laugh, and when I laugh I can't play tag."

"I won't tag you with my crutch," spoke Uncle Wiggily with a laugh. "Now we're ready to begin."

So the little duck girl and the rabbit gentleman played tag there in the woods, jumping and springing about on the soft mossy green carpet under the trees.

Sometimes Lulu was "it" and sometimes Uncle Wiggily would be tagged by the foot or wing of the duck girl, who was a sister to Alice and Jimmie Wibblewobble.

Before Uncle Wiggily could stop himself he had run into the bush.

"Now for a last tag!" cried Uncle Wiggily when it was getting dark in the woods. "I'll tag you this time, Lulu, and then we must go home."

"All right," agreed Lulu, and she ran and flew so fast that Uncle Wiggily could hardly catch her to make her "it." And finally when Uncle Wiggily almost had his paw on the duck girl she flew right over a bush, and, before Uncle Wiggily could stop himself he had run into the bush until he was half way through it.

But, very luckily, it was not a scratchy briar bush, so no great harm was done, except that Uncle Wiggily's fur was a bit ruffled up, and he was tickled.

"I guess I can't tag you this time, Lulu!" laughed the bunny uncle. "We'll give up the game now, and I'll be 'it' next time when we play."

"Ail right, Uncle Wiggily," said Lulu. "I'll meet you here in the woods at this time tomorrow night, and I'll bring Alice and Jimmie with me, and we'll have lots of fun. We'll have a grand game of tag!"

"Fine!" cried the bunny uncle, as he squirmed his way out of the bush.

Then he went on to his hollow stump bungalow, and Lulu went on to her duck pen house to have her supper of corn meal sauce with watercress salad sprinkled over the sides.

As Uncle Wiggily was sitting down to his supper of carrot ice cream with lettuce sandwiches all puckered around the edges, Nurse Jane Fuzzy Wuzzy looked at him across the table, and exclaimed:

"Why, Wiggy! What's the matter with you?"

"Matter with me? Nothing, Janie! I feel just fine!" he said. "I'm hungry, that's all!"

"Why, you're all covered with red spots!" went on the muskrat lady. "You are breaking out with the measles. I must send for Dr. Possum at once."

"Measles? Nonsense!" exclaimed Uncle Wiggily. "I can't have 'em again. I've had 'em once."

"Well, maybe these are the French or German mustard measles," said the muskrat lady. "You are certainly all covered with red spots, and red spots are always measles."

"Well, what are you going to do about it?" asked Uncle Wiggily.

"You must go to bed at once," said Nurse Jane, "and when Dr. Possum comes he'll tell you what else to do. Oh, my! Look at the red spots!"

Uncle Wiggily was certainly as red-spotted as a polka-dot shirt waist. He looked at himself in a glass to make sure.

"Well, I guess I have the measles all right," he said. "But I don't see how I can have them twice. This must be a different style, like the new dances."

It was dark when Dr. Possum came, and when he saw the red spots on Uncle Wiggily, he said:

"Yes, I guess they're the measles all right. Lots of the animal children are down with them. But don't worry. Keep nice and warm and quiet, and you'll be all right in a few days."

So Uncle Wiggily went to bed, red spots and all, and Nurse Jane made him hot carrot and sassafras tea, with whipped cream and chocolate in it. The cream was not whipped because it was bad, you know, but only just in fun, to make it stand up straight.

All the next day the bunny uncle stayed in bed with his red spots, though he wanted very much to go out in the woods looking for an

148

adventure. And when evening came and Nurse Jane was sitting out on the front porch of the hollow stump bungalow, she suddenly heard a quacking sound, and along came Lulu, Alice and Jimmie Wibblewobble, the duck children.

"Where is Uncle Wiggily?" asked Lulu.

"He is in bed," answered Nurse Jane.

"Why is he in bed?" asked Jimmie. "Was he bad?"

"No, indeed," laughed Nurse Jane. "But your Uncle Wiggily is in bed because he has the red-spotted measles. What did you want of him?"

"He promised to meet us in the woods, where the green moss grows," answered Lulu, "and play tag with us. We waited and waited, and played tag all by ourselves tonight, even jumping in the bush, as Uncle Wiggily accidentally did when he was chasing me, but he did not come along. So we came here to see what is the matter."

The three duck children came up on the porch, where the bright light shone on them from inside the bungalow.

"Oh, my goodness me sakes alive and some paregoric lollypops!" cried Nurse Jane, as she looked at the three. "You ducks are all covered with red spots, too! You all have the measles! Oh, my!"

"Measles!" cried Jimmie, the boy duck.

"Measles? These aren't measles, Nurse Jane! These are sticky, red berries from the bushes we jumped in as Uncle Wiggily did. The red berries are sticky, like burdock burrs, and they stuck to us."

"Oh, my goodness!" cried Nurse Jane. "Wait a minute, children!" Then she ran to where Uncle Wiggily was lying in bed. She leaned over and picked off some of the red spots from his fur.

"Why!" cried the muskrat lady. "You haven't the measles at all, Wiggy! It's just sticky, red berries in your fur, just as they are in the ducks' feathers. You're all right! Get up and have a good time!"

And Uncle Wiggily did, after Nurse Jane had combed the red, sticky burr-berries out of his fur. He didn't have the measles at all, for which he was very glad, because he could now be up and play tag.

"My goodness! That certainly was a funny mistake for all of us," said Dr. Possum next day. "But the red spots surely did look like the measles." Which shows us that things are not always what they seem.

And if the—Oh, excuse me, if you please. There is not going to be a next story in this book. It is already as full as it can be, so the story after this will have to be put in the following book, which also means next.

Let me see, now. Oh, I know. Next I'm going to tell you some stories about the old gentleman growing cabbages, lettuce and things like that out of the ground, and the book will be called "Uncle Wiggily on The Farm." It will be ready for you by Christmas, I think, and I hope you will like it.

And now I will say good-bye for a little while, and if the lollypop doesn't take its sharp stick to make the baby carriage roll down the hill and into the trolley car, I'll soon begin to make the new book.